T0067124

I MEAN YOU NO HARM;
I SEEK YOUR GREATEST GOOD

OTHER BOOKS BY JIM MEEHAN

Hearts Have Reasons (UK Outword Trust 1995; USA Thomas Moore 2000)

Reasons Have Hearts Too (UK Outword Trust 1997; USA Thomas Moore 2000)

Sugar Free Sweet Talk (USA Talent Plus 2009)

Hall Ways to Success and Significance (USA Talent Plus 2013)

I MEAN YOU NO HARM;
I SEEK YOUR GREATEST GOOD

Reflections on Trust

Jim Meehan

I MEAN YOU NO HARM; I SEEK YOUR GREATEST GOOD REFLECTIONS ON TRUST

Copyright © 2015 Jim Meehan.

All rights reserved. No part of this book may be used or reproduced by any means, graphic, electronic, or mechanical, including photocopying, recording, taping or by any information storage retrieval system without the written permission of the publisher except in the case of brief quotations embodied in critical articles and reviews.

Send all inquiries to:
Jim Meehan - j007meehan@aol.com

iUniverse books may be ordered through booksellers or by contacting:

iUniverse
1663 Liberty Drive
Bloomington, IN 47403
www.iuniverse.com
1-800-Authors (1-800-288-4677)

Because of the dynamic nature of the Internet, any web addresses or links contained in this book may have changed since publication and may no longer be valid. The views expressed in this work are solely those of the author and do not necessarily reflect the views of the publisher, and the publisher hereby disclaims any responsibility for them.

Any people depicted in stock imagery provided by Thinkstock are models, and such images are being used for illustrative purposes only. Certain stock imagery © Thinkstock.

ISBN: 978-1-4917-6149-6 (sc)
ISBN: 978-1-4917-6150-2 (e)

Library of Congress Control Number: 2015905893

Print information available on the last page.

iUniverse rev. date: 04/24/2015

To
Maureen,
Larissa, Hamdi and Amir

Trust is the lifeblood of all good relationships with self and others – and not just close personal relationships.

Trust or Bust

What when absent makes a relationship go bust?
What if not found means a relationship is lost?
What is not only desirable, but also a must?
The cementing ingredient is mutual trust.

Jim Meehan

CONTENTS

LIST OF ILLUSTRATIONS

Photographs

Figures

Maps

PROLOGUE

"I woke up one morning with a tune in my head and I thought, 'Hey, I don't know this tune – or do I?' It was like a jazz melody. My dad used to know a lot of old jazz tunes. I thought maybe I just remembered it from the past. I went to the piano and found the chords to it (a G, F# minor 7 and a B), made sure I remembered it and then hawked it round to all my friends, asking what it was: 'Do you know this? It's a good little tune, but I couldn't have written it because I dreamt it… It didn't have any words at first so I blocked it out with 'scrambled eggs.' 'Scrambled eggs, oh my baby, how I love your legs-diddle, diddle- I believe in scrambled eggs.'"

Paul McCartney
The Beatles Anthology 2000

The tune had come into Paul's mind while he slept at the family home of his girlfriend, Jane Asher, in Wimpole Street, London. However, the final lyrics and title came several months later. During a brief holiday in Portugal at the villa of Bruce Welch, a guitarist with the Shadows pop group, the song we know as "Yesterday" finally evolved. Shortly after his return to England, Paul went to Abbey Road studios in London on June 14, 1965, and in two takes recorded his solo version of the work. George Martin later dubbed in a string quartet, and "Yesterday" subsequently became a track on The Beatles album *Help*, which was first issued on August 6, 1965, in the United Kingdom. In the United States, the song was released as a single and quickly reached number one in the record charts and today is still the most played tune on American radio.

My wife, Maureen, pointed out to me that this is not an uncommon experience. She told me that the story of Frankenstein was taken from a dream its author, Mary Shelley, had. She dreamt about a scientist who attempted to create a living human being but ended up constructing a monster.

Having composed several poems, something similar has happened to me on occasion. One such occurrence relates to the title of this book. In 1991, I had moved to Atlanta, Georgia, in the United States to work with an eminent American psychologist, Dr. William E. Hall. One of his areas of expertise was human relationships, and he maintained that mutual trust was at the heart of all good relationships. Five years later, while visiting him in Omaha, where he was then living with his wife, Susan, in sheltered accommodation, he asked me to consider what attitudes people need to have in order to create mutual trust. Around the same time, I was putting together a collection of poems to give to my mother for her eightieth birthday.

During this period, I recall waking up one night just after midnight. Restless and unable to fall back to sleep, I got up, made my way to the kitchen, brewed a cup of coffee and sat at my desk. With a cup of coffee in one hand, I picked up a pen with the other and, in a contemplative mood, started doodling on a yellow legal paper pad. After filling the page with scribbles, drowsiness returned; half asleep, I returned to bed and soon dropped off into a deep slumber. Later that morning, fully rested and revitalized, I made my way over to my desk, picked up the pad and examined the contents with interest. In the top left-hand corner, five words caught my notice, "I mean you no harm," so I put a circle around them. Diagonally opposite in the bottom right-hand corner, another five words stood out, "I seek your greatest good," so I circled them. I then joined the two circles with a thick black line, thinking that they could be useful ingredients of a poem. However, on further reflection, I began to see that the ten words were two promises that expressed the key attitudes that a person needed to have in order to create trust. At last I had found an answer to Dr. Hall's quest.

These ten words became the refrain of a poem composed in April 1997, which in its final form was entitled "Total Trust." Dr. Hall was a pioneer of positive psychology, so the poem is an attempt to link trust and a positive approach to life.

Total Trust

I mean you no harm;
I seek your greatest good.
Come, take me by the palm,
We'll see the stars not just the mud.
We'll see the doughnut not just the hole.
We'll walk that extra mile,
And adopt a more positive role.
No longer half dead, but fully alive.

I mean you no harm;
I seek your greatest good.
Come, take me by the arm,
We'll understand, then be understood.
We'll find ourselves in each other,
And lose ourselves there too.
The mystery of "I" – "other,"
One entity, yet two?

I mean you no harm;
I seek your greatest good.
In cold weather, I'll keep you warm.
When hungry I'll give you food.
My life is filled with calm,
As it is fully understood,
Yes...
You mean me no harm,
You seek my greatest good.

From time to time after making presentations on relationships or leadership or after reciting poems, a member of the audience will ask me where the mantra "I mean you no harm; I seek your greatest good" came from. Somewhat glibly, I would typically respond, "I'm not sure," or "I haven't the foggiest idea." Sometimes I would defensively answer the question with a question: "Where do composers get their notes from or painters their images or poets their words?"

Interestingly, when reading Ruth Ozeki's novel *A Tale for the Time Being*, nominated for the Man Booker Prize and The National Book Critic's Circle Award, I came across a passage in which one of the characters asks, "Where do words come from?" The character then continues, "They come from the dead. We inherit them. Borrow them. Use them for a time to bring the dead to life...The ancient Greeks believed that when you read aloud, it was actually the dead, borrowing your tongue, in order to speak again...The Island of the Dead. What better place to look for missing words... Sweet dreams." Although I was not sure where the ten words came from, I soon found out that the words had legs and were going places, as the following episode illustrates.

Eight or nine years ago, while enjoying a coffee break in my office in Lincoln, Nebraska, I was absorbing the majestic panoramic view. The office overlooked several golf course greens nestled under the arch of a big sky with the silhouette of the state capitol and other buildings breaking the distant horizon. Suddenly, I was grounded by a telephone call. It turned out to be an old boy whom I vaguely remembered from Saint Philip's Grammar School in Birmingham, United Kingdom. He was not one of my inner circle of close friends. He was checking out a reference to a certain Jim Meehan that appeared in a book he was given during a management conference he had attended in Shanghai. The book, *The Speed of Trust,* was written by Stephen M.R. Covey, son of the famous Stephen R. Covey, author of the international best seller *The 7 Habits of Highly Effective People.* The caller, whom I had not seen since 1959, told me that while he was reading the book on his return flight to the United Kingdom, he had noticed quotes from icons like Albert Einstein, Mahatma Gandhi and Winston Churchill. Then, suddenly, the pattern was broken by the inclusion of an unknown British psychologist and poet, Jim Meehan. Flabbergasted, he wondered if it could possibly be the boy who was in his year at grammar school.

"Is that you?" he asked in excitement.

"The name and titles I own," I responded, but added, "However, I haven't come across the book, so you will need to read the actual reference."

He then proceeded to read the quotation.

"Having spent many years trying to define the essentials of trust, I arrived at the position that if two people could say two things to each other and mean them, there was the basis for real trust. The two things were, 'I mean you no harm; I seek your greatest good.'"

Totally surprised, I admitted that the reference was correct. We finished our conversation by discussing how he obtained my US business telephone number and agreed that we must get together the next time we were both in England.

Later that same day in the materials department at work, I noticed a parcel containing copies of *The Speed of Trust*, which were to be circulated to heads of department. Before leaving work, there was a copy on my desk with a note of congratulations inscribed from our then president, Kimberly Rath. What a remarkable coincidence and proof positive that the ten word mantra has legs.

In April 1997, when the poem now known as "Total Trust" was first penned, I was fifty-four years old and certainly had harmed a number of people both intentionally and unintentionally in different ways. In no way would I like to give the impression that I am guilt free, nor have I always sought everyone's greatest good. I have put a few people down in my time. When Alexander Pope wrote "To err is human," he was right on the mark. Although there are people I dislike and with whom I disagree, nevertheless, I can assure them that I mean them no harm and seek their greatest good.

While training for the 2012 Chicago Marathon, which involved a lot of solitary running, I began to think more seriously about the question, "Where did the ten words come from?" This book started off as my attempt to answer that question. After several possible contributing factors were put forward, including cultural issues and the influence of five mentors, other questions arose. These questions related to the actual meaning of the words, how meaningful are they to others, and consideration is given to their momentum and possible destinations. The book then turns into my attempt to respond to these matters. Just as the ten words became the opening refrain of the verses of the poem "Total Trust," the book contains an epilogue with other examples of my attempts to capture concepts and feelings concerning total mutual trust and related topics in verse.

Human beings, to use a metaphor, are like volcanoes, every now and then erupting with varying degrees of intensity.

I hope you enjoy the lava flow.

MY YESTERDAYS

By a strange coincidence, I was born in the same year, the same city, the same hospital, and in the same ward as the famous Beatle Sir Paul McCartney. Not only do we have the same birth address, Walton Park Hospital, 107 Rice Lane, Liverpool North, but we have the same first name, James, and the same registrar, W.S. Bailey. Paul was born on June 18, 1942 and yours truly was born on September 20, 1942. Moreover, McCartney's father, Jim, and my father, John, worked in a local aircraft factory. Jim was a center-lathe turner, and my father was a timekeeper. Apart from being fans of early rock and roll singers like Buddy Holly and the Crickets and Eddie Cochran, that is where the similarity with Paul ends. I am still an admirer of the music of The Beatles and of Paul McCartney. For my seventieth birthday, my wife, Maureen, bought tickets for a show of his that was held in St. Louis, Missouri, in November 2012. Two years later on July 14, we went to see him perform in Lincoln, Nebraska. He and his band were great!

As a psychologist, I am aware of the difficulties relating to the reliability of childhood memories and their factual accuracy. Even eyewitness testimonies are notoriously flawed, and these witnesses recount their perceptions very close to the time of the incident. Looking back over sixty-nine or so years is far more hazardous. What distinguishes imagination from memory is that memory is locked into a definite time and space. However, when tracing childhood mental images, we are often faced with a stream of consciousness rather than totally episodic events. Sometimes we have reconstructed events influenced heavily by the anecdotes of others who tell us their interpretation of situations in which we were players. What we then commit to memory are the reconstructions of events, which often make good stories.

John and Margaret Meehan on their wedding day
July 21, 1939 and their second son, James, five years
later at the age of one year and ten months.

In his book *Travels with Epicurus*, Daniel Klein has a chapter titled "On Solitary Reflection" in which he discusses the benefits old age provides when it comes to thinking. He cites views of many philosophers, ancient and modern, a few poets and of the psychologist and existential philosopher Erik Erikson. He notes, "An inherent problem in writing one's memoirs for others to read is the temptation to indulge in literary nips and tucks. After all, who really wants to be remembered as, say, a man who spent an inordinate amount of time watching *Law & Order*? Not for publication!" Klein is persuaded by Erikson and writes, "Erikson says that mature and wise ways of reminiscing are precisely what we need in an authentic old age...Tying our experiences together in a personal history is a way we find meaning in our lives...Even when we are only composing memoirs for ourselves alone, we cherry pick our memories, choosing those that give us some semblance of a neat narrative line to our personal histories, some sense of cause and effect, even of personal growth."

In answer to the question, how do we know what is real and true? Klein concludes, "Indeed the fact that I have this memory and attach significance to it matters more than its absolute, objective truth," adding the disclaimer, "no, I am not wandering off into la-la-land where I claim a memory is true simply because I think it is true." He then goes on to relate that "a series of lectures on the art of memoir held at the New York Public Library was called Inventing the Truth. Cute, but they were also onto something important with the title: when we try to put together our life story, we seek out patterns and themes, and that, in turn determines which memories make the cut. And of course, the other way round too: we sift through our memories for themes and then search for memories that validate them."

In his stimulating book *Subliminal,* Leonard Mlodinow, a social neuroscientist, devotes a whole chapter to remembering and forgetting. He writes, "the unconscious tricks that our brains employ to create memories of events – feats of imagination, really – are as drastic as the alterations they make to the raw data received by our eyes and ears. And the way the tricks conjured up by our imaginations supplement the rudiments of memory can have far-reaching – and not always positive – effects." He outlines how the two-tiered human brain, made up of conscious and unconscious elements, can create memories and explains why we sometimes remember what never happened.

Despite the challenges presented in giving accurate accounts of recalled events, I will try to be as objective and as authentic as I can be in selecting situations and experiences that have influenced or contributed to the creation of the ten-word mantra that dropped onto the page in the nineties.

Certainly, 1942, the year I was born, was a very violent time in Europe, and many people were causing great harm to others. Indeed, 1942 was the midpoint of World War II, which began in 1939 and did not end until 1945. My father was conscripted early in the war as private, number 1057478/R.A.O.C., and served throughout hostilities, including a long period in Mechelen, Belgium. Interestingly, I know within a day or so when I was actually conceived. My father was given three days' leave on Christmas Eve, Christmas Day and Boxing Day in 1941. Nine months later, almost to the day, yours truly was born.

After the war, bombed building sites, or "bombies" as they were called by locals in Liverpool, littered many landscapes and were used mainly by children as playgrounds. Liverpool and surrounding areas were the most heavily bombed districts in the country outside of London. Reports were deliberately kept low key to hide the real damage from the Germans. My mother, Margaret, known affectionately as "Pearl" or "Pearlie" by her family, was evacuated at the beginning of 1941 to Southport, a coastal resort almost seventeen miles north of Liverpool. Southport is better known for The Royal Birkdale Golf Club, which has hosted the Open Championships on many occasions. There, she give birth to my elder brother, John, on May 27. Just as well, because in the period between May 1 and 7, 1941, by all accounts, 681 Luftwaffe bombers attacked and over 2,000 lives in Liverpool were lost. 6,500 homes were completely demolished and a further 190,000 were damaged. For a couple of years, my mother, brother and I lived with my aunt Ellen, whose house was next to a "bombie." Two of the neighboring houses on one side had been destroyed by fire caused by incendiary bombs landing on their roofs. Bombed building sites were not the only reminders of war. Outside my aunt's house, there was an air raid shelter in the middle of the street that was in ruins, smelled of urine and was a gathering place for vermin. Not far away on the beaches of Seaforth and Blundelsands, cement blocks had been constructed in order to obstruct possible German troop landings. Each child in our area had a tin helmet and a gas mask to wear. My brother, John, and our friends had great fun playing with what we thought were toys.

Although my mother and father were both born and raised

in the Liverpool suburb of Seaforth, by the time they met as adults, my father's family had moved up the social ladder somewhat. My paternal grandfather, also named John, had progressed from being a general laborer working at the Liverpool dockyards to a supervisory position. This enabled him to move his family to Aigburth, a very well appointed district with two beautiful parks. Sefton Park was tastefully landscaped, had lakes, a horse gallop trail and a bird aviary. Otterspool Park contained picturesque nature walks and was being expanded to provide a promenade with scenic views of the River Mersey. My grandfather's wife, Mary, did not work, as she had a number of serious health issues. My father's family could be described as lower middle class.

My father was the third child. Stephen, an older brother, died at birth, and Edward, better known as Eddie, was a year older than my father. The fourth and final child, Mary, was several years younger than my father. My father and Mary were well educated. My father went to St. Francis Xavier's College where, among other subjects, he learned French, which was instrumental in his posting to Belgium during the war. For health reasons, Eddie could not travel overseas, so he became a member of the Home Guard. The day after I was born, Mary married John Heuston, who was posted shortly afterward to North Africa. The war touched everyone.

My mother's family remained in Seaforth. My maternal grandfather, Philip, better known as Phil, was a stevedore at the docks. His hands were permanently clawed as a result of the continuous use of a hook that hung from his belt. Daily he would stand in line and wait to be picked to help load or unload a ship. Failure to be selected meant no work, no pay and no food for the family table the following day. His wife, Lucy, worked in a local laundry. My mother's family was working class.

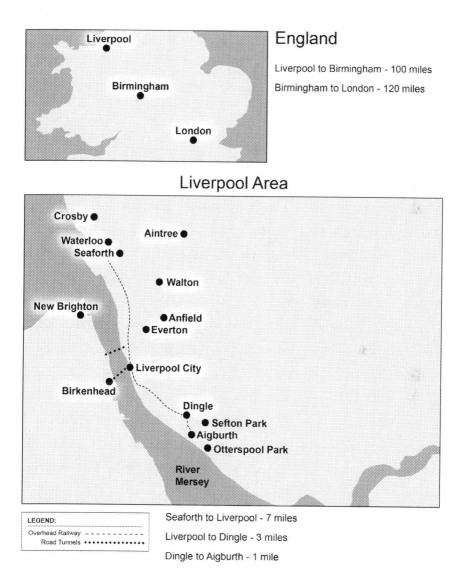

England

Liverpool to Birmingham - 100 miles

Birmingham to London - 120 miles

Liverpool Area

LEGEND:
Overhead Railway - - - - - - - - - - -
Road Tunnels ••••••••••••••

Seaforth to Liverpool - 7 miles

Liverpool to Dingle - 3 miles

Dingle to Aigburth - 1 mile

By a strange coincidence, my mother's maiden name was Bond, and the first name on my passport is James. As such,

I developed a certain affinity with the name James Bond. I read one or two of Ian Fleming's books about the man "with a license to kill" while at school and watched a couple of movies based on his novels, too. However, I would have preferred him to have a license to wound or indeed "a license to help others to grow." Many people think my personal email beginning j007meehan is precocious, but jmeehan was already spoken for!

My mother was the eldest of the eight children in her family. When she was born, she was stone deaf in her right ear and 'nervously deaf' in her left ear. This meant that whenever she was afraid or uncomfortable, she was unable to hear through that ear. For all intents and purposes, she was treated as a sort of deaf-mute person who could not speak properly. The family did not have the financial resources to have her condition diagnosed or treated. At school she learned little and spent her time putting out the slates, chalk and cleaning cloths and changing the water for flowers. She had her knuckles slapped by the very strict nuns if she tried to join in the singing because she made unusual noises. She learned to read lips, make signs and words and even read to some extent. Often she would surprise people by playing tunes by ear on an old piano, which was well used at the parties held at the Bonds' house.

After my mother left school, she followed in her mother's steps and worked for a while in a local laundry before taking up a service role in a well-to-do house in nearby Waterloo, a resort for posh people, where she first met my father. My father was attracted not only by her looks but by her reserved manner and the fact that she was not very talkative. Just before they married in 1939, my mother was living with her maternal aunt Ellen who welcomed her company, particularly as Ellen, a spinster, was afraid of ghosts.

While my father was overseas contributing to the war effort, life was not full of total peace and harmony for my mother, who needed help to raise a family. For my parents, buying a house was simply out of the question. My father wanted my mother, my brother and me to live in Aigburth with his family in a sort of commune. My mother soon became uncomfortable being away from her family, friends and familiar places. Moreover, she could not engage in lengthy conversations with my paternal grandparents and their children, who were more sophisticated than she was. My mother was naturally gregarious but was often reduced to play the role of a 'shrinking violet' at social gatherings. Yet, she valued her independence and disliked being told what to do, as if she were a child. I noticed that to gain attention, sometimes my mother would be quite contrary. Her preference was to live in Seaforth where her own family and neighbors constantly praised her for what she did and for what she achieved. Accordingly, there were often misunderstandings and disagreements between the adults, which resulted in much change and upheaval. Considerable time was spent by our family as we shuttled between Aigburth and Seaforth, which were on opposite sides of the city. It all depended on who would put us up, or, rather, who would put up with us.

This was the world in which I grew up and these were the key players with whom I shared the stage. This was my normal. I felt valued by family members who gave me a lot of independence from a very early age. My mother was an excellent companion who enjoyed playing cards and board games and always tried to win. She particularly liked games of chance, such as betting on the football (soccer) pools and betting on horses, which in those days was illegal if it involved placing bets outside the boundaries of the racecourse. She could carry out these pastimes on a solitary basis, although she would often ask me to take her wagers to the illegal "bookie's runner" who operated from a coal shed in one of the nearby houses and also to collect any winnings from him. Gambling after the war was seen in the United Kingdom as the poor person's opportunity to become rich quickly. There was a greyhound racing stadium in Seaforth that my father and mother visited. My father, my uncle John and my uncle Eddie taught my mother how to place bets and use numeric tables to calculate her winnings. She learned her lessons well; until the day she died, she would try to have a small daily "flutter" on the horses as it is called in England. In 1961, 'off-course' betting shops were made legal in Britain. Even in my father's short period of retirement, I would often see him crunching numbers, as he was convinced there was a mathematical way to break the betting system used at greyhound racing tracks and provide him with a steady return on his investments, or should I say bets? Once or twice he persuaded me to go with him to the Hall Green greyhound racing track in Birmingham to help him place bets. Sometimes he would win a little, but more often he would lose a little. He enjoyed the effort but never to my knowledge created a winning formula.

I looked forward to the times when my maternal grandfather would take me with him to the docks. We would board the overhead railway, the first in Europe, which traveled for seven miles, sixteen feet above the ground, past all the docks, the Pier Head and the famous Liver building as it made its way between Seaforth and Dingle. Often we would disembark at a station, explore the neighborhood and possibly board a vessel. I recall visiting Gladstone dock, the biggest dry or growing dock in Europe at the time, with the biggest water gates. My grandfather would also take me on the ferry across the Mersey to the seaside resort of New Brighton or to the shipbuilding yards at Birkenhead. My aunt Ellen also took me with her often to the city center to visit the markets and the Catholic cathedral where she would attend Mass. She enjoyed walking with me and her dog, Spot, to Crosby to spend time with relatives. My aunt Mary would often let me join her when she went to have afternoon tea with her friends who lived in grand houses in the vicinity of Aigburth. She and her husband, John, would enjoy challenging me with riddles and conundrums. Uncle John also took me to football (soccer) matches and to horse races. I have fond memories of going with him to the Aintree National Hunt Racecourse in Liverpool and sitting on his shoulders to witness arguably the greatest steeplechase in the world, the Grand National. It is approximately four and a half miles in length and has 30 demanding fences that serve to test the best horses and jockeys. Certainly my early childhood world was a world in which no one I knew meant me any harm, and all the key players sought my greatest good.

On my seventieth birthday party in England, I was pleasantly surprised when presented with a red book entitled *This is Your Life* and slightly embarrassed when many friends recounted anecdotes and said nice things about me. My elder brother, John, a priest, could not attend. He had agreed many months before to lead a parish pilgrimage to Lourdes in the south of France. He had kept the week of my birthday clear, but I could not be in the United Kingdom until September 29, more than a week after my birthday. The master of ceremonies for the celebration, Paul Harris, who authored the red book, amused the audience with the following excerpt:

> Your brother John recalls the early years of your lives in Liverpool...when actually you saw very little of your father. He was mostly absent during the war and this continued even after the war with his work. You moved constantly between your grandparents at one end of Liverpool and your other grandparents at the other end of the city. Never really settled, therefore John recalls the amount of freedom you both enjoyed due to the absence of your father. In fact, John remembers that you were quite a handful and told me about one particular instance when you were about three years old. Due to the war, you were living with three or four families under one roof and you would all gather for Sunday dinner at a long table with everyone, including you, dressed in their Sunday best. On this particular occasion, this meal was presided over by your grandfather.

John recalls how you were standing on your chair with your hands on the table in an effort to dominate the proceedings. (At this point, Paul adds to John's original script, "A trait I'm told that continues up until this day!") Unhappy with your behavior, your uncle Eddie told you to sit down and behave yourself. Not happy with his request, you threw a potato at him across the table and registered a direct hit – quite impressive for a three-year-old. Needless to say, you did not get to finish your dinner that day...

This story was total news to me. I have no recollection of the event. John is sixteen months older than I, so his recall of this time is a lot clearer than mine. Certainly the "potato incident" does not support the view that as a child I was totally opposed to violence and that such pacifism contributed to the formulation of the promise "I mean you no harm." Yet, it could be argued that the age of three falls well short of the accepted age of reason, that is, the developmental stage when children become accountable for their decisions and actions.

However, as I grew older, images of war would not go away. My mother and my aunt Mary used to take John and me to the cinema. Pathé News would often show newsreels of bulldozers moving piles of bodies at German Nazi concentration camps. These images of the aftermath of war were totally incomprehensible to me. But the violence did not end there, as most popular films involved fighting between cowboys and Indians, and cops and robbers. Many of the games kids played reflected these films. I did not enjoy playing such games, much preferring sports such as football (soccer) and cricket, both team games.

The only war I knew was one that erupted on occasion on the streets of Seaforth, where gangs would have raiding parties and fights. Plum Street would fight Date Street. The kids would throw or catapult stones and clay balls at each other and take hostages. Sometimes, despite our protestations, we would be forced to take sides. I found this violence very distasteful and meaningless. Nor did I like the pub brawls that broke out on rare occasions as we waited for mum who was "having a Guinness" with her parents in a local pub. It was known that those involved were drunk or out of their minds, though this was not the case with thugs who were members of those street gangs. Certainly I was averse to violence. My ideal world was one in which people would help, not harm each other.

Our Lady Star of the Sea elementary school in Seaforth admitted me at four years of age. Spending time at school was a totally new experience, requiring much adjustment. After school, I would explain to my mother what was learned and she enjoyed learning it as well. My mum was keen to learn and a quick learner, too. Because she was not nervous when with me, she could hear whatever was said. Her vocabulary increased, and she began to read other columns of the newspaper besides the section on horse racing and football results. We even tried simple crosswords. However, there were some words that she found hard to pronounce. For instance, we had two types of milk, sterilized and pasteurized, and they had different bottles. The former was kept in long, thin bottles with a metal bottle top, and the latter in short, fat bottles with a cardboard press-on top. We reached a simple solution. We called sterilized milk "goat's milk" and pasteurized milk "cow's milk." Some words she used like appetite sounded more like "apple tart" when Mum pronounced them. School friends and visitors found our communication system strange, but, at a practical level, it worked. Our own personal language solidified our family relationships.

There was one particular teacher at school whose lessons I enjoyed immensely. She would read poems to us and Aesop's fables, stories from the Arabian Night's Tales and the fairy tales of the Brothers Grimm and Hans Anderson which fascinated me, even though some of them contained violence. Unfortunately, there was an element of violence that occurred at school which today would be regarded as child abuse. Some pupils, including me at times, were given the cane or had their knuckles rapped with a ruler for making what I considered to be minor mistakes or for being what the teachers considered to be insubordinate when it appeared to me often to be no more than a child's confusion or lack of understanding. Yet another form of meaningless violence! In addition, the priests and nuns used to put the fear of God into us and told us that if we died with the stain of a mortal sin on our soul, we would go straight to Hell and burn for all eternity.

One year, the school priest and my school teacher were presented with a moral problem by yours truly. During Lent, they gave each pupil a Good Shepherd card. On the front was a picture of Jesus tending to a flock of poor people. On the reverse side there was a cross with 60 squares on it. Pupils were encouraged to collect a penny for each box and put a cross in the square to keep score of the money collected. To make the exercise interesting, there was a prize for the first completed card. Mine was handed in first together with the five shillings collected (equivalent to 25 pence today, not taking into account inflation). However, it was discovered that I had taken some of my aunt Ellen's gas meter money without her knowledge and I was shamed for cheating and stealing. The teacher told my mother that in some countries they would have cut my hand off for such a deed. I was somewhat surprised, as the teacher was very enthusiastic when she read the story of Robin Hood, who was a British folk hero who stole from the rich to help the poor. It seemed to me that he was harming the rich to seek the greatest good of the poor serfs. So why the double standard? Was taking from the poor to help the poorest of the poor a mortal sin? Many Hail Mary's were recited as penance for such a serious transgression after I confessed the incident to the parish priest! Maybe the teacher needed to explain that Robin Hood thought he was giving back to the poor what was rightfully theirs and not stealing from the rich but taking back from them. It was quite confusing to me at the time. Whose greatest good was being sought, mine or the poorest of the poor? Certainly it was not my aunt Ellen's!

As children, we were told by our elders that the Roman Catholic Church was the one true Church and that Protestants were rebels who had screwed up. So Catholics and Protestants fought like cats and dogs. Yet another form of meaningless violence! This form of sectarian divide even carried over to sports. My elder brother John was taken to

Goodison Park as a young boy by his paternal grandfather to see the Catholic team Everton play. In the early days of the club, some directors openly supported Home Rule in Ireland. I was taken by my uncle John to Anfield Road to see Liverpool play, even though he was actually a keen Everton supporter. Liverpool was regarded as the Protestant team. Soon after the club was formed, some of its directors showed an interest in Masonic affairs and supported Unionist views. Today there is less sectarianism, but when I was a boy, it was fairly widespread. To this day, my brother and I keep our allegiance to our soccer teams. At The Orient, a pub in Speke, Liverpool, the Everton supporters, dressed in blue and white, keep to their side of the premises and Liverpudlians, dressed in red and white, keep to their side. Both sets of supporters keep their memorabilia and collectibles on show. Despite their rivalry, nowadays the fans maintain a harmonious relationship. Many modern authors go so far as to say the sectarian divide between the reds and the orange and the blues and the green is a myth, but I experienced it as real.

While my aunt Ellen was very generous and very supportive, there were occasions when severe differences and misunderstandings arose between her and my mother. At times they could erupt into fighting and physical violence. On one occasion, John and I were sitting on the stairs cheering for my mother, who was screaming as my aunt was pulling at her hair. My mother swiveled and at the same time pushed my aunt through the open kitchen door into the backyard, whereupon she locked the door. At this point, I came down the stairs and went to look out of the kitchen window to see what my aunt would do next. Unfortunately for me, she picked up a mop bucket and threw it through the window in a rage. Interestingly, my brother John recollects that it was my mother who threw the bucket. In any event, a shard of glass flew into my hand and blood started gushing out, which brought the fight to an end. The glass was removed, the wound was cleaned, iodine was poured on the area, which caused it to sting a great deal, and it was bandaged with some cloth. When questioned at school about my injury, I told the truth and explained what had happened. That evening the parish priest visited the house and reprimanded my mother and aunt in no uncertain terms. There were no sweets for me for several weeks for informing on my aunt. Though such events were rare, they were very frightening when they happened. I wished that my mum and aunt could have sat down and talked the matter through rather than resorting to violence. But what did I know? I was only five years old.

By the time my father was finally demobilized, there were very few suitable jobs left in Liverpool, so he went south a hundred or so miles to Birmingham, England's second largest city. It is known as the capital of the Black Country, the industrial heartland of England. His brother, Eddie, lived there and was a conductor on the Birmingham Corporation public buses. He helped my father to obtain similar employment.

One Saturday morning, shortly before we were due to move to Birmingham to join my father, I was sent on an errand to Aigburth Vale Co-operative butchers to collect some sausages and meat. One of the games I played as I walked along was to throw my school cap high into the air and catch it. As I crossed the tram lines, I threw my cap into the air and it perched on top of a pole supporting the overhead wires. Immediately I shimmied up the pole, but on reaching out for my cap, a tram went by and my mind went blank. I awoke the following Tuesday in the Children's Hospital in Liverpool City Centre asking for pork sausages and a joint of beef. I was told that I received an electric shock, fell off the pole, bounced off the roof of the toilets in the Vale twenty or so feet below and landed on the ground in a state of unconsciousness.

One night while I was recovering in the hospital, there was a great commotion. A stretcher brought in a patient who was heavily bandaged and surrounded by doctors and nurses. Later I learned that it was a boy who had been stealing lead from the roof of the Liverpool Anglican cathedral and had fallen from a great height. Unfortunately, he died. I thanked my lucky stars that the team of doctors and nurses had been able to keep me from harm and had helped me regain consciousness.

Liverpudlians have a distinct form of humor. Among other things, they nicknamed the Liverpool Catholic Cathedral "Paddy's Wigwam," which is both a reference Irish Catholics and the architectural form of the building. Many Liverpudlians jokingly refer to Liverpool as the capital of Ireland. Someone once remarked that people needed a sense of humor to live there. Certainly, I found the graffiti very amusing, and every family and community group, including the school classroom, had a comic or comedian among its members. My maternal grandfather was full of quips, including one that amused me. He used to say, "Our family was so poor, we used to keep a pig in the corner to act as an air freshener!" After I was discharged from the hospital, a friend told me that a boy knocked on our front door which my mum answered. The boy shouted, "There's something wrong with your Jimmy's head."

"I know," my mother said and shut the door.

She probably did not hear him properly, but the story got around.

Birmingham Area

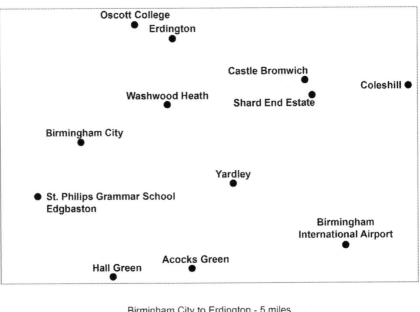

Birminham City to Erdington - 5 miles

Birminham City to Edgbaston - 2 miles

Birminham City to Acocks Green - 5 miles

Once again, my brother John has a separate version of events. He recalls meeting some members of a local gang to which he belonged and telling them that I was in hospital and that there was something wrong with my head. The gang members said something to the effect that there had been something wrong with my head for quite some time before the accident!

After I was discharged from hospital, my father took my mother, brother and me to live with him in Birmingham. He had rented some rooms in Yardley, a pleasant suburb five or so miles from the city center. The house backed onto a canal. It is a little-known fact that within the boundaries of Birmingham City, there are more miles of canals than in Venice, Italy. Although we only lived in Yardley for a couple of years, several events contributed to my development during that period. My brother John and I had been enrolled in the local Catholic school, Sacred Heart and Holy Souls, in the suburb of Acocks Green. The Holy Souls referred to those spirits who had died without a mortal sin and thereby avoided the clutches of Hell, yet they had committed some venial or minor sins that had not been forgiven at the time of their death, which required that they had to suffer in purgatory for a time in order to be cleansed before being allowed to enter heaven. This seemed to be a scary and strange state of affairs to me as a child.

In order to help us become part of the community, my father encouraged John and I to become members of societies. We joined the Cub Scouts and I also became an altar boy and joined the Guild of Saint Stephen to learn how to help the priest during his celebration of the Mass. These roles were service roles and provided us with the opportunity to take on more responsibility, including some supervisory roles. The other children at school thought we talked with a peculiar accent, as the Liverpool dialect used more high tones and Liverpudlians tended to speak through their noses.

In particular, the local children laughed when we pronounced words such as "square," "fair" and "work," which they said sounded like "squaw," "fur" and "wirk." John and I laughed at the way they pronounced words such as "five" and "you," which sounded to us as "fah-yeef" and "yow" as in cow.

The most disconcerting experience for me at Holy Souls School was being ordered by a teacher to put on boxing gloves, ostensibly to learn pugilistic skills. Fortunately, my opponent knocked me out in the first round. I explained that I was susceptible to concussions following my accident in Liverpool and that was the end of that exercise for me. To this day, I have found the so-called sport of boxing to be senseless because it harms others. Brains and other bodily organs are inevitably damaged in the activity.

Up to this time, for me, school had been a routine chore. There was a lot of unnecessary monotonous repetition and learning by rote. At the age of four, I had to learn the Catholic Catechism by heart. When asked by the priest "Who is God?" I replied, "A supreme spirit who alone exists of himself," which I still do not fully understand today. Monday to Friday, children went to school. Some found it easy and got ticks and stars, and others found it difficult and merely got crosses and probably made the teachers cross. I had experienced little difficulty with lessons, and, apart from one teacher who read poetry and stories to us, I was neutral toward teachers who, to me, had a job to do. After school, pupils had time to play. I used to like going to the library when it was raining or was bitter cold to peruse books and read magazines that our family could not afford. Saturday and Sundays were usually days to play sports or watch others play.

On June 17, 1951, my younger brother, Stephen, was born. Birmingham City Council allocated houses to rent on the basis of numbers of family members. Soon after Stephen's birth, we were given the keys to a brand new house in a modern housing development on the outskirts of the city in the suburb of Shard End. So once again, we had to move. We took up residence in Brownfield Road. My mother and father lived in this house until they died. My father went first in May 1976 at the age of 66, and my mother followed in April 2001 at the age of 83. While we lived there, my younger sister, Margaret, was born on February 19, 1955. Apart from four and a half years at college, I lived there until getting married to Maureen in 1971.

Shard End, being a newly constructed housing estate, had no Catholic school or church. For educational purposes, Catholic children had to be shuttled by privately chartered buses to and from a neighboring suburb, Erdington, some five or so miles away. My brother John and I were put on the register of Saint Mary and Saint John's Infant and Junior school. As an eight-year-old child, the daily commute seemed to be a major journey that was lengthened by numerous pick-ups in the mornings and drop-offs in the late afternoon on return. At school, we were known as the "Shard-Enders."

My experiences in Liverpool and Birmingham during my early formative years provide certain possible clues to the source of the two promises, "I mean you no harm; I seek your greatest good." Despite the "potato incident" and the "good shepherd" conflict of values episode, could they have their roots in my early childhood aversion to senseless violence, unjust war and unnecessary conflict, not to forget the sectarianism which was so rampant? These experiences in Liverpool and Birmingham represent a transition from images of war, uncertainty and violence into a period of peace, stability and hope of a better future. Certainly, I had developed an abhorrence for senseless injury to others and unnecessary harm, which could take many different forms, and a dislike of activities that promoted negative people outcomes. A good part of the answer to where the words came from lies in the power of the positive relationships in my life, especially the one I had with my mother. However, I would like to explore the relationships built with some special people, other than family members and close personal friends, who have had a positive influence on my life. People who truly brought out the best in me – my mentors. These mentors certainly meant me no harm and sought my greatest good.

MENTORS MATTER

In the *Odyssey*, Homer tells how Odysseus (otherwise known as Ulysses, the king of Ithaca) before setting off for the Trojan Wars instructed his faithful companion, Mentor, to raise his son, Telemachus, to become fit to ascend to the throne as his successor. Interestingly, this Greek myth also introduces female involvement, as the Greek goddess of wisdom, Athena, at one point assumed the disguise of Mentor to guide the young Telemachus as well.

Homer, writing c.700 BC, probably chose the name Mentor because in Greek its roots lie in the word "counsel" or "mind." There is a sense of protecting or of being a "minder" and also a sense of being a "developer." The protective aspect of the role has given rise to the use of the term "protégé," taken from the French verb *protéger*, which means to protect, to refer to the recipient of a mentor's efforts. Mentor and Telemachus were not the first mentor and protégé in history, but they do provide an example of an enduring positive relationship by which a wise and experienced person can bring out the best in a less experienced and less mature individual.

Nowadays, the traditional or classic model of mentoring is being called into question. In an interesting article titled "The Misery of Mentoring Millennials" with the subtitle "Younger workers are shunning the one-on-one mentorship model of the past in favor of a social network," the writer,

Marina Khidekal, assesses the relevance today of seeking out a single career confidant, which she sees as old fashioned. In the article, she quotes Jeanne Meister, co-author of *The 2020 Workplace*, who wrote "Millennials can be bold and hungry when it comes to getting what they want... Today's new mentorship models are more like Twitter conversations than the long-term relationships of days past. They're short term and quite informed. And they end before it becomes a chore for either party – like moving on from a just OK date." She goes on to describe new approaches in companies such as "peer mentoring" or "reverse mentoring" in which older workers are mentored by younger workers who are more au fait with new technologies and social media, or "speed-mentoring" in which protégés face off individually with prospective mentors, speed-dating style.

However, in the same publication, in the article "Just the Two of Us," David Westcote states that "Until Millennials came along, one-on-one mentorships seemed to work just fine." He goes on to list six powerful one-on-one mentoring/protégé relationships to include Socrates and Plato, Aristotle and Alexander the Great, Joseph Hayden and Wolfgang Amadeus Mozart, Andrew Carnegie and Charles M. Schwab, Mary Alice Duncan and Oprah Winfrey, and Larry Summers and Sheryl Sandberg (Facebook COO).

My view is that individuals require many mentors over a lifespan, some short term and others longer lasting, to fit mutual needs, and that different models will be required for different people, but that one-on-one mentoring will endure across generations. Psychologists are aware from research studies that mentors often learn and benefit more than protégés from the mentoring relationship.

Although Mentor was formally requested by Odysseus to take up the role, not all mentoring relationships are so structured; some may arise more spontaneously. Sometimes these relationships start on a formal or even on a contractual basis related to achieving set targets, but then turn into deep friendships and the focus widens to broader life goals and even to life's purpose. In such cases, there is an element of serendipity or unintended consequences. It is as if the people power in a relationship begins to ignite and the mentor and protégé find that they like each other, have mutual interests, spend quality time with each other and both begin to flourish. While we can learn much from people we respect but dislike, we always learn more from people we both like and respect. Liking is the switch that moves a formal relationship of mutual respect into a mentoring relationship. Both parties mean each other no harm and seek each other's greatest good, and the power of total mutual trust is unleashed. Such was the case in the mentoring relationships I have experienced. Mentoring relationships, like all other human relationships, have to be continually cultivated or nourished, otherwise they break down. Human beings can often harm each other inadvertently and have to work with each other to resolve misunderstandings and use their mutual trust to do so. In my search to discover where the words "I mean you no harm; I seek your greatest good," came from, it occurred to me that they reflected, in part, my experiences of powerful mentoring relationships.

MORE THAN A TEACHER

When my brother John and I arrived at Saint Mary and Saint John's school, it was only a few weeks before the end of the summer term, so we were put together into the top junior class, which was run by a teacher named Mr. Keene. Right from the start, he drew my attention. He appeared to me to be younger than other teachers who had taught me. He welcomed my brother and me into the class in a friendly manner. There was something about his style that seemed different. He maintained a strict discipline based on respect rather than shouting or acting as a dictator. He managed to keep the attention of most of the pupils most of the time by involving them, asking questions and encouraging fellow pupils to give them answers. He split the class into groups to work on specific projects but allowed some pupils to work on special assignments on their own. He let each child work at his or her own pace, and he tailored tasks to meet pupils' abilities, but always stretched them. To me, it was like a breath of fresh air. He opened my eyes to science and the world of astronomy. He challenged me with geometry, he taught me calligraphy and helped me develop a personal freestyle of writing. I looked forward to going to school for the first time.

In 1956, two years after I had left to go to St. Philips
Grammar School, Saint Mary and Saint John junior school
soccer team beat Nechells 1-0 to win the Plaza Cup.

Top row left to right adults: Mr. Keene (coach), Mr. Heneghan
(headmaster) and Mr. McGuire, Saint Mary and Saint
John's School Staff members. Bottom row, center: Holding
the ball is Paul Lawrence who provided the photo.

Mr. Keene encouraged me to read about people who had
changed the world, composers such as Wolfgang Amadeus
Mozart and Ludwig Van Beethoven, poets such as Alfred
Lord Tennyson and William Wordsworth and scientists such
as Louis Pasteur and Albert Einstein. On later reflection,
after studying Greek culture, Mr. Keene seems to me to be

like Plutarch the Greek philosopher, priest and historian of the first century AD who encouraged people to use good role models as patterns to copy or as standards against which to monitor their own behavior. Plutarch realized that, left to their own devices, humans imitate each other. He wanted to create exemplars of virtue for young people in particular to emulate. It also helped that Mr. Keene was from Liverpool and spoke, like me, with a heavy accent.

It was a great disappointment when the school term ended and we had to go on a six-week break for the summer holidays. After the recess, my brother was sent to secondary school at Saint Thomas Moore and Blessed Edmund Campion, also in Erdington, about a mile and a half or so from Saint Mary and Saint John's school, to which I returned. To my dismay, because of my age, I had to join junior three, which was the class before Mr. Keene's. I was devastated to have to wait a year to go into his class.

The class teacher for junior three was a straight-laced elderly woman who was very rigid and proper. Back we went to traditional routines, like sitting upright with our arms folded. She had to shout in order to keep order, and, as soon as her back was turned, certain troublemakers would take advantage. If she caught them, they would be publically punished, which she hoped would deter such behavior. However, to me it seemed merely to increase it, as the troublemakers often wanted attention, and she certainly put the spotlight on them. She stuck rigidly to the curriculum and exercises in our textbooks. I thought I would be better off going to a library or staying at home to read the textbooks and just go to school to take tests. I was bored out of my mind at school, where everything was prescribed and predictable. In English language classes, she was more interested in grammar, spelling and punctuation than content and style. There was only one right answer that was acceptable to her. "Green as grass" received a tick, but "green as a seasick baby" was given a cross. She spent little time with pupils who could cope and gave most of her resources to slow learners. I felt she cared little for me as a person, and a sense of mutual mistrust built up between us. Toward the end of what I could only at best describe as a stagnant year, our mutual distrust came to a head.

One morning after the pupils had been given their daily mini-bottle of pasteurized milk and were filing back to their desks, the girl in front of me dropped the lid from the top of her milk bottle onto the floor. The teacher noticed it and without any enquiry accused me of being a "litter lout" and ordered me to pick it up at once. As I had not dropped it and the girl who had was frightened to admit it, I refused. The teacher exploded and commanded me to pick it up and place it in the waste bin. Again I refused, as I had not dropped it and still had my own bottle top in my hand. At this point, she went ballistic and took me to the headmaster's office, telling me that for such insolence and insubordination, Mr. Heneghan had grounds to expel me from the school. She and the headmaster threatened that if I did not go and pick up the bottle top, there would be serious consequences. Once more, I refused on the grounds that I did not drop it and no attempt had been made to establish who was guilty. In the final analysis, they decided to isolate me from the rest of the class and put me and my desk on a stage at the back of the classroom where I remained quite content until the summer recess. Outside the classroom it was back to normal, playing with the friends who stuck with me during this period. To this day, I do not know who actually picked up the bottle top. All I know is that at the time, I was convinced that the teacher meant to harm me and certainly felt that she did not seek my greatest good. However, thinking back, she probably thought blind obedience was called for and that I meant her harm and failed to seek her greatest good. She operated on the basis of total control and probably would have instructed me to water telegraph poles to prove her power. I would probably have refused and been put back into isolation again!

In September 1952, I was overjoyed to be able to rejoin Mr. Keene's class and prepare for the "eleven plus" public examination. This examination had been introduced into the final year of elementary schools in United Kingdom in 1944. If a child passed this test, he or she would proceed to a grammar school to be prepared for later entry into professional traineeships or university. If a child did not sit the examination or failed to meet the standards required, he or she would proceed to a secondary school to be prepared for trade apprenticeships or secretarial or administrative courses of training and education.

I knew Mr. Keene must have known about "the bottle top" incident, but nothing was said, and he continued to teach me as before without any noticeable difference. With his help, I progressed in geometry to calculating the volumes of objects, including cylinders. He arranged for me to make an architectural plan or layout of the school to scale and encouraged me to enter several international writing competitions. He gave me books of questions concerning general knowledge to complete in my own time and gave me a book of answers so that I could mark my own work and proceed at my own speed. He asked me to lead a team working on an exciting project relating to the depiction of the ceremonies and pageantry relating to the coronation of Queen Elizabeth II, which took place on June 2, 1953. He encouraged me to study the history of public transport over the previous hundred years from the time that George Stephenson and his son Robert built an early steam engine, *Rocket*, in 1852 right up to the manufacture of modern buses, trams and trolley buses. He kindly took me to witness the final journey of Birmingham's official last tram, the number 2, which passed by our school as it traveled from Steelhouse Lane, in the Birmingham City Centre, to Erdington on July 4, 1953. Mr. Keene also included me in the football (soccer) and cricket teams, which involved travel after normal school hours, and he encouraged me to participate in athletics, particularly running longer distances. All in all, he had the ability to engage the other pupils and me by finding out about our interests, and he stretched and pushed us to raise our standards. When I had to sit for my eleven plus examination for entry to St. Philips Grammar School in Edgbaston, he told me that I had nothing to worry about. Thanks mainly to him, I managed to pass, and a new world of academic opportunity was opened up.

Although I visited Mr. Keene and his family to say thank you after completing my philosophy course at college, I do not think he really fully appreciated the positive impact that he had on my life. I know he genuinely meant me no harm and that he sought my greatest good.

MORE THAN PRIESTS

When we moved to Shard End, there was no Catholic church building, but there was a Catholic priest, Father Thomas Whittle, who had a presbytery in Hurst Lane, which was at the east end of the road on which we lived. He had moved to the parish in 1950 and looked to expand its borders to cover the newly formed Shard End Housing Estate. Father Whittle was an Irishman and had an Irish pedigree retriever that he called Shot, a beautiful golden-haired dog. He had the air of a country gentleman, well suited to business negotiations and spending time hunting and golfing.

The presbytery was a small town house with a garage attached and was situated at the junction of Hurst Lane and Longmeadow Crescent. Mass was said every morning in the downstairs front room and the sacristy was the downstairs lounge at the rear of the house. On Sundays, Mass was performed at the nearby community center in Castle Bromwich village, and Christmas Eve Mass was held in the Bradford Arms Public House! Land was purchased not far from the presbytery and a target was set to build a church dedicated to Our Lady the Mother of God and Guardian Angels with an infant and junior school attached. A standalone presbytery was also envisioned to be built in Kitsland Road to complete the complex.

As a trained altar boy, I used to get up each morning

before seven o'clock, make a cup of tea for my mother and go to 'serve Mass.' This was followed Monday through Friday by school. As the parish grew, there was an opportunity for another priest to help out. Indeed, Father Whittle wrote to Lord Archbishop Bright on September 2, 1953 to pursue a possible candidate:

> Some little time ago, I was speaking to Canon Flint. He told me that he was getting a new curate, and that Fr. O'Callaghan was leaving Coleshill... I spoke to Fr. O'Callaghan telling him I could find work for him in Castle Bromwich providing he could get your Grace's permission. He was not too eager as he considered the Parish too residential than a slum Parish. I had a letter from him recently saying he would come if permission was given him, but he would prefer some place where there was a church and school.
>
> If he comes, he must be prepared to rough it. The accommodation is very limited. The presbytery is small; two downstairs rooms, one of which is used as a chapel; a kitchen, two bedrooms and a box room. I recently acquired a permanent housekeeper, one of us therefore would have to occupy the box room. Next year we shall have more room as we hope to have the church built by then, thus freeing the room now used as a chapel.

On October 3, 1953, Father Whittle once more wrote to Lord Archbishop Bright to press for a curate. He stated:

> Father O'Callaghan is with me at the moment. He supplied for me during my holidays. I would be most grateful if you would give me permission to keep him.
>
> The position here is somewhat desperate. We have close on 2,000 in the parish. The Hall we use for Sunday Masses only accommodates 150. This Hall is the local community centre and the only one available in the area. Many of the parishioners travel long distances to other churches for Sunday Mass... Those who come, we pack in as best we can but there is great discomfort and the people overflow onto the roadway. Some stand outside by the windows and try to attend Mass that way. Two more Masses would relieve the situation and help us to get the benefit of our numbers...
>
> Father O'Callaghan has settled in very well, he does not at all mind crush and inconveniences. Now that he knows the people, he is most anxious to stay. I have found him a very good worker, naturally good at visiting.

I beg your Grace to give favourable consideration to my request.

FATHER DAVID O'CALLAGHAN

One morning, a new priest, Father David O'Callaghan, had arrived to say Mass. He too was Irish. His hair was going gray and he seemed to be very nervous, somewhat on edge and a worrier. Any slight noise or movement seemed to annoy him and break his concentration. During Mass, he was so intent on being liturgically correct that he appeared to be scrupulous or neurotic. However, after Mass, when he had put his vestments away and after I had cleared the altar and put my cotta and cassock away, he began a friendly conversation to find out all about me and was very grateful for my help. He was the total opposite in many ways to Father Whittle in the way he carried himself and in his manner of dress, which was not fashionable. His shoes were well worn, his trousers were shorter than they should be, and under his black jacket, which was slightly blacker than his more outworn trousers, he often wore a gray pullover that had small holes in it. He was rarely entirely clean shaven. He was from County Cork, Eire, and his Irish accent was very pronounced. He was the salt of the earth and had no airs and graces. He was different. He was human. He was approachable. He was humble. He was frail. He was vulnerable.

On Monday through Friday, I had to rush off to school after Mass. On Saturdays and Sundays, we would chat a little more. I discovered that he had been a missionary priest, a member of the Order of Saint Francis Minor (O.F.M.) who had been sent to China, where he served the people for eighteen years. He told me that he had been involved in The Long March, which took place during the time of Chairman

Mao. He related that it was so cold on the walk that he wore seven shirts, and when he sweated too much he would take off the bottom one, wash it and put it back on top. He told me of his time in prison and how he had been put in solitary confinement and how he was taken out every so often and put in a grave expecting to be buried alive. He let me know how much he loved the Chinese people, especially the peasants who had nothing. He informed me that he'd had a nervous breakdown and had been expelled from the country and was sent to our Archdiocese to rehabilitate. His stories, to me, were enchanting, and the more stories he told, the more I admired his courage and generosity.

Over time, he became a familiar member of the community as he cycled in all kinds of weather to visit Catholic families. He often wore a beret, French style, and had his trouser bottoms tightened by bicycle clips or tucked into his socks. You could tell Father O'Callaghan was in the area, as his bicycle would be propped up against a gate, post or tree next to the house, shop, garage or café he was visiting. Many times he would come to our house and have a cup of tea. He would give my mother a few shillings, as she was finding it difficult to make ends meet. He never made a fuss and was accepted as a friend. He recruited my brother and me to collect waste paper and cardboard and take it to be bundled and sold to raise money for his favorite charity, Father Hudson's Homes, which looked after orphans. It was located four or five miles away in the small town of Coleshill.

Once I saw Father O'Callaghan pedaling his bike in the snow with a small table strapped to his back. When he saw me, he stopped for a quick chat, during which he told me he was on his way to the orphanage to drop off the table a generous parishioner had given him. As he pushed off to cycle against the wind and the snow along a route that was not exactly level, he made a great impression on me. He persuaded John and me to sell raffle tickets by going door to door. In addition, he asked me to persuade families to take a collection box into which they could place coins. All proceeds were then sent to overseas missions. Once a family accepted a box, it was my job to visit the family every so often, empty the box, give them a receipt and deliver the money to a parish organizer, who banked it. Father O'Callaghan kept me totally occupied, what with serving daily Mass and being asked to attend Benediction and Rosary evenings on Sundays and Wednesdays. Often, as a reward for my efforts, he would take me to see my favorite Midlands soccer team, West Bromwich Albion, who were playing amazingly well at the time. It was a long journey from Shard End to the Hawthorns Stadium, the home ground of the football club, and this meant taking two bus rides, which gave Father O'Callaghan more time to tell me more stories about his time working as an Irish missionary priest in China.

One particular incident involving Father O'Callaghan made a lifelong impact upon me. While serving Mass, he genuflected many times, and I noticed that he had a hole in the heels of his socks. I decided to put money aside and buy him a pair of good socks for a Christmas present. As my daily commute to and from St. Philips Grammar School involved changing buses at Birmingham City Centre, I decided to visit city stores to see what was being offered in the way of men's socks. Wolsey provided the best offer, as they had on sale woolen socks with heels reinforced with nylon, but they were the most expensive. I saved every penny I could and managed, on the last day of school in 1954, to buy a pair of these high-class socks. It gave me great pleasure to wrap them up and leave them in the sacristy for Father O'Callaghan. After serving Mass on Christmas Day, I was putting my cotta and cassock away and saw Father O'Callaghan giving the socks I had bought him to a poor person who looked like a tramp. It seemed extraordinary to me that someone who obviously needed something could see someone more in need and make such a sacrifice. Not only did Father O'Callaghan preach that it was better to give than to receive, he actually practiced what he preached. Maybe, I thought, one day I could be like that and become a priest.

Father David O'Callaghan celebrating the Nuptial Mass for the wedding of Anne McGrath and Jim Cusack in 1962 at Our Lady Mother of God and Guardian Angels Parish church Castle Bromwich.

While conducting the final edit of the manuscript for this book, my brother Steve and I met Kevin McGrath in Birmingham. Kevin and Steve were close friends as teenagers and recently bumped into each other at Kevin's golf club, which Steve was visiting. During a brief conversation, they arranged to meet and Kevin promised to provide a photograph for publication in the book he heard I was writing. It shows Father O'Callaghan as the celebrant at the Nuptial Mass during which Kevin's sister, Anne, and her husband, Jim Cusack, married each other. On a visit to the United Kingdom at the end of August 2014, Steve asked me to join him and Kevin for a reunion in Birmingham to exchange some memories. When we talked about the "socks incident," Kevin remarked that his mother, who is ninety-five years old and still going strong, told him many similar stories. In particular, he recalled his mother telling him that the women of the parish took pity on Father O'Callaghan because his woolen jumper was full of holes. They raised money to buy him a new one but were somewhat surprised to discover that he continued to wear his old one because he had given his gift to someone whom he felt needed it more than he did.

My father, who was a devout Catholic, had bought a set of Butler's *Lives of the Saints*, which he paid for over a period of years. Following the "socks incident," I began to read all about saints who exemplified a life of sacrifice. Some saints, like Simeon Stylites, seemed crazy to me. He achieved fame for living on a pillar for thirty-seven years in Aleppo, Syria. However, there were many more down-to-earth people who worked tirelessly to help others, like Saint Don Bosco, who was one of my favorites. Some of the stories about saints were very similar to fairy tales I read as a child. Sometimes the line between fact and fiction was hard to fathom, but the challenge of exploring their lives was very stimulating at the time. Once again, the influence of Plutarch's cult of heroes can be seen in the teaching of the Catholic Church, as it draws on the lives of its saints to create role models. We become who we imitate. While this happens at a subconscious level, we can also consciously choose the models we want to emulate to bring out the best in us. Not that my father was aware of the influence of Plutarch in what he was doing.

On the practical side, I tried to emulate these role models. From time to time, I use to accompany Father O'Callaghan on the Midland Red bus to Coleshill to visit and play with the orphans at Father Hudson's Homes. We also visited Saint Gerard's Children's Hospital and spent time talking to patients, some of whom were in "iron lungs," massive machines that helped them to breathe. It did not take me long to realize that a lot of children were not as fortunate as I was.

As I moved into my teenage years and became interested in girls and pop music, my focus changed somewhat, and Father O'Callaghan was transferred to another parish, Saint Joseph the Workman in Bidford-on-Avon twenty-five miles away. Accordingly, our lives drifted apart. Maureen and I went to visit him at the General Hospital in Stratford-Upon-Avon shortly before he died on December 27, 1975, at the age of sixty-five. This gave me the opportunity to express my gratitude for his friendship, the positive impact he had on my life and the help he gave to my family. Father David O'Callaghan was someone who meant me, and others, for that matter, no harm and continually sought our greatest good.

In March 2005, I was given the opportunity to spend some time with a client in Shanghai. As the plane was beginning its descent, I recall looking out of the window and thinking back to the days I spent with Father O'Callaghan. Never in my wildest dreams did it cross my mind that I would visit China and meet the people whom he thought were very special. It was a very poignant and emotional experience, and tears began to roll down my cheeks. A flight attendant approached me with tissues in her hand and asked if something was ailing me. As I dried my cheeks, I told her that a deceased friend of mine had spent much time in China. Little did she imagine that he was imprisoned and among the many missionaries who served the Chinese people and were finally banished from the country. It was surprising to me that his memory would impact me so deeply. When asked by my hosts in Shanghai what I would most like to do socially during my stay, they were startled when I asked to be taken out into the country and visit a village where it was possible to eat with ordinary people and share their company. As I ate my dumplings, the locals looked on in astonishment. For some of them, it was probably the first time they had seen a white man, let alone eaten with one. Just as Father O'Callaghan had described, they were very polite as they bowed and smiled profusely.

Recently, when surfing the web, I came across an article written on November 6, 1970, in *The Catholic Herald*, a United Kingdom newspaper, under the heading "Sanguine Feat," quoted in full below:

Father David O'Callaghan, parish priest of St. Joseph the Workman, Bidford-on-Avon, Warwickshire, was recently presented by the Lord Mayor of Birmingham with his Blood Transfusion Gold Badge to mark the donation of the 50th pint of his blood.

This is not the first "thank you" that Father O'Callaghan has received. During his 18 years in China before being expelled by the communists in 1948, he was presented with a white silken banner by grateful Chinese Buddhists whom he had helped to feed during the Japanese invasion.

For his part in dissuading the Japanese from extracting reprisals against innocent villagers, he was given a "Wan Min San" ("10,000 Peoples Umbrella"), one of the highest Chinese honours.

He received a second honour when he persuaded the Japanese to allow transplanting of rice shoots in one country area, thereby averting starvation.

The more I reflect on his life and my good fortune to be counted among his close friends, even for a short period, the more grateful I am to have met someone who lived the mantra "I mean you no harm; I seek your greatest good."

FATHER GEOFFREY WAMSLEY

Before joining Saint Philip's Grammar School, Father David O'Callaghan had asked me to consider studying for the Catholic priesthood. So when I settled down at the new school, I joined a group dedicated to pursuing that purpose, "The Curé D'Ars Society," named after Saint Jean-Marie Baptiste Vienney, who was a French priest from the parish of Ars. He is the patron saint of parish priests. The society was run by Father Geoffrey Wamsley, the school chaplain, a gentle, pious and warmhearted gentleman who was very well read but did not really have the toughness of temperament necessary to manage rowdy schoolboys and keep order. Society meetings were more orderly and held within the Oratory church adjacent to the school. We studied the life of the Curé D'Ars and visits were arranged to local seminaries and monasteries to meet and talk to students about their experiences. Many of the students had been pupils at St. Philips.

My early teenage years were somewhat turbulent and rebellious. As a result, I decided to drop out of the Curé D'Ars Society, much to the regret of Father Wamsley, who asked me to reconsider and urged me always to keep in touch. My quest to establish independence clashed with my father's wishes to keep me under control. He was very strict and tried to limit the time I spent with friends going to dances and youth clubs, preferring that I stayed at home to study. Rock and roll was all the rage at the time. The movie *Rock Around the Clock,* featuring Bill Haley, was banned in Birmingham because of riots and fights between "Teddy Boys," who wore "drainpipe" trousers reminiscent of those worn in Edwardian days and thick suede shoes, and their rivals, who were dressed in a more conventional style. However, Castle Bromwich was outside the Birmingham city limits at that time, and the Castle cinema in our neighborhood showed the movie, attracting troublemakers from far and wide. I remember going to the "Kwik" café opposite the cinema to listen to the jukebox. "Blue Suede Shoes," written by Karl Perkins and sung by Elvis Presley, and his other top-ten hit, "Heartbreak Hotel," were played most of the time. Buddy Holly and the Crickets were my favorite singers. I would encourage customers to play "That'll be the Day" and "Maybe Baby," as I had no money to put in the jukebox. It is interesting to note that John Lennon got the idea of The Beatles from Buddy Holly's backing group, the Chirping Crickets, which calls to mind the sound of American insects. Lennon chose common English insects, beetles, and changed the spelling to "Beatles."

My father justifiably accused me of wasting much of my time. He disapproved of me going to the West End Cinema in Birmingham to see the film *The Girl Can't Help It*, which starred Jayne Mansfield, a well-endowed blonde actress with an hourglass figure. I genuinely went to see Gene Vincent, Eddie Cochran, Little Richard, Fats Domino, the Platters and Julie London, who gave amazing performances. My father took down my photos of the actress and model Brigitte Bardot, who was known as the "French sex kitten." He disapproved of my hairstyle, which was combed back in waves; he asked me to brush it down when we went to church as if I were a choir boy. He was amazed when I became a part-time hair dresser's model and made it to the finals of the Brylcream

Hairdressers Cup held in Birmingham. He let me participate because the barber, Mr. Foley, was a Catholic parishioner who also lived on Brownfield Road. Tension was so strong between us that I spent the six-week summer holidays one year with my mum's relatives in Liverpool, as they were more relaxed and less critical.

Pop music was a major interest in my life, so when Buddy Holly, Ritchie Valens and a singer known as "The Big Bopper" died in a plane crash in northern Iowa on February 3, 1959, it acted as a wake-up call for me. Devastated, I began to think of the frailty of life and the need to use and not waste time. Plutarch would have been proud of me, as I returned to reading the lives of famous people who had made the most use of their time, reread the life of Mozart and began listening to his music. Next I studied Beethoven, whose music I enjoyed more because in it he seemed to me to express the full range of human emotions; this was followed by an examination of some of the works of Tchaikovsky. The music of Dvorak, especially pieces influenced by folk music, led me to the works of American composers like Aaron Copland and Leonard Bernstein and the songs of Joan Baez and Bob Dylan, who sang in the style of his idol Woody Guthrie. My awareness of the power of songs to express individual sentiments and make social comments broadened considerably.

My father was relieved as I returned to my studies and did well at my public examinations, enabling me to proceed to the sixth form, which prepared students for higher education. My strongest subjects were mathematics, physics and chemistry. An educational psychologist advised me to consider a career in engineering or architecture. However, I was undecided, as people and their problems interested me more. For me, poetry is a form of architecture in words.

During a pivotal period in the autumn term of 1959, I decided to play safe by choosing pure and applied mathematics, physics and chemistry as my major areas of interest. I also opted to take general studies in order to widen my horizons. Such topics as the philosophy of Hegel and how his ideas of dialectic materialism influenced Karl Marx and led to the formation of communism kept me occupied. I compared communism to early forms of Christianity and other contemporary communities such as the Essenes, who were mentioned in the Dead Sea Scrolls and to whom many think John the Baptist had an allegiance.

Another experience that challenged my faith occurred at that time. A teacher from Czechoslovakia (now the Czech Republic), a country behind the Iron Curtain, visited our sixth form for a year or so. He taught us the rudiments of the Russian language and introduced us to the poems and writings of Boris Pasternak and Alexander Pushkin. He described the possibility of living in a totally materialistic society at peace with nature and fellow citizens. During this period, I read some of the writings of Lenin as well as *The Communist Manifesto* and *Das Capital* by Karl Marx, who had written "religion is the opium of the people." Marxism maintained that institutionalized religion served to control the masses of people for the benefit of the rich and was not in the interests of the working class.

Many other ideas challenged my Catholic faith, and I decided to talk to Father Geoffrey Wamsley again. Father Geoffrey was an admirer of Cardinal John Henry Newman, who had converted from Anglicanism to the Catholic Church in the late nineteenth century. So impressed was he with the life and legacy of Newman that he, too, converted from the Anglican Church to the Roman Catholic Church in 1941.

Father Geoffrey Wamsley

Father Geoffrey was a very learned and humble man who had studied at Oxford University and gained a first-class honours degree in theology in 1933 and progressed to vice principal of Cuddesdon College in Oxfordshire. He entered the Birmingham Oratory in 1942, a religious community set up by Newman.

The 'Oratorians,' as they were known, were followers of

Saint Philip Neri, a notable Roman prelate. In 1945, Father Geoffrey was ordained to the priesthood and became a teacher and chaplain at St. Philip's Grammar School. Newman was one of the founders of the Oratorian Order in the United Kingdom. Newman, moreover, was a great apologist or defender of the Roman Catholic faith with an interest in the formation of a Catholic University in Dublin, where he helped to establish University College.

Father Geoffrey was much sought after as a spiritual director and just the person with whom to spend some time. He was delighted to talk to me; he greeted me like a prodigal son and listened to my doubts. He introduced me to the works of Newman, many first editions of which were in the library at the Oratory. In particular, he encouraged me to read *Apologia Pro Vita Sua*, a defense of his religious opinions, and *The Dream of Gerontius*, which was put to music by another Roman Catholic, Sir Edward Elgar, whose music I studied and whose talent I revered. His "Enigma Variations" and "Cello Concerto" are included in my favorite pieces of music to this day. Father Geoffrey not only directed my reading, but he also encouraged me to live a life of faith, attend Mass regularly and carry out good works. He was renowned for his good deeds. Like Father David O'Callaghan, Father Geoffrey Wamsley worked tirelessly for the poor and needy, at times eighteen or more hours a day. Living out his instructions, I began to consider once more exploring a vocation to the Roman Catholic priesthood. If I could find answers to life's questions, this would make me happy, and I could make others happy, too, was my way of thinking. He encouraged me to rejoin the Curé D'Ars Society, where I reconnected with a former classmate, Eddie Butler, who has since become a lifelong friend.

It was interesting to learn that Eddie's sister, Teresa, was in the same class at the same secondary school in Erdington as my elder brother, John, and that Gerard, one of Eddie's brothers, was in the same class as my younger brother, Steve, at Archbishop William's secondary school in Tile Cross, Birmingham. Eddie had an unwavering vocation to the priesthood, stuck it out, became ordained and retired a few years ago to live in Ireland. We often traveled together on the bus home from school and talked about issues.

At this time, Father Geoffrey encouraged my visits to All Saints Hospital in Birmingham, a mental institution, to spend time with an adult who had a form of schizophrenia. Due to his condition, he could not be looked after by his elderly parents, who lived in our parish. I would escort him to and from home and take him for walks. Bernard was his name. He was a wonderful human being. Father Geoffrey also decided that during the Christmas holidays of 1959, Eddie and I should go on a short retreat to Manresa, a Jesuit house in Roehampton, London, to see if we should follow our vocations into the priesthood. The retreat was conducted by Father Leonard S.J., who had worked as a missionary in Rhodesia, Africa, now Zimbabwe, which he described as the Garden of Eden. He concluded that we should continue in our endeavor.

In January 1960 on return to St. Philips, I changed my majors to history, French and Latin, and kept general studies. My father was relieved and pleased with the direction in which my life was moving, as was my mother.

For the next eighteen months, Father Geoffrey acted as my spiritual director. However, our lives soon gradually drifted apart as I pursued my religious vocation in all seriousness by enrolling in Grove Park Seminary in 1961, a branch of Saint Mary's College, Oscott. My studies lasted over four and a half years before terminating in the spring of 1965, just about the same time that Paul McCartney was trying to make sense of "scrambled eggs, oh my baby, how I love your legs, diddle, diddle – I believe in scrambled eggs," which became "Yesterday."

The four and a half years spent as a seminarian introduced me and my fellow students to the world of philosophy. Not only did we study Greek philosophers, beginning with Thales of Miletus, but every distinguished Western philosopher up until modern thinkers like the existentialists Soren Kierkegaard, Jean Paul Sartre and Martin Heidegger; Alfred North Whitehead and his process philosophy; the analytic philosophers Bertrand Russell and his protégé Ludwig Wittgenstein and the logical positivism of Sir A. J. "Freddie" Ayer. In addition, we studied a system of philosophy known as Thomism, which involved learning logic, epistemology, metaphysics, ontology, cosmology and philosophical psychology. Our eyes were opened to the history of the Old Testament and the history of the Roman Catholic Church in the Western Civilization. I had the opportunity to study other religions such as Islam, Confucianism, Hinduism, Buddhism, Daoism, The Church of The Latter Day Saints, Scientology and various Christian movements including the Pentecostalists, who speak in tongues, and those seeking Rapture at the end of days.

In the summer of 1963, I was in Rome and experienced the excitement of students for the priesthood who were witnessing the proceedings of the Second Vatican Council, which had commenced in the previous October. Certainly, at the Villa Palazzolo, the summer residence of the students of the Venerable English College, major changes in the teachings of the Catholic Church were expected on such matters as divorce and the use of contraceptives, in the practice of the liturgy with respect to the use of local languages and in more scholarly approaches to the interpretation of the Bible. I recall the breathtaking views across Lake Albano to the Papal residences below at Castel Gondolfo, where Pope Paul VI resided at the time. On one visit to the Papal Palace, I met a group of North American students for the priesthood, one of whom was from Saint Joseph's Seminary, Yonkers, New York, a certain Peter Meehan, who turned out to be a distant cousin of mine on my father's side. He is now pastor of the Church of the Holy Rosary in Manhattan.

During my time in Rome, doubts about my true vocation in life began. I found dogmatic theology stimulating because it used philosophy to try to explain ideas such as the Trinity, three persons in one divine nature, or the hypostatic union, how Jesus could be God and man, that is, be both one divine person with two natures, one divine and one human. When it came to questions of moral theology and the prospect of directing the personal lives of others on medical matters and sexual practices, I was not so comfortable. Finally, I concluded that the priesthood was not the life for me, nine months before the Second Vatican Council was called to a close in December 1995.

Without the wisdom, counsel and support from Father Geoffrey, that wonderful journey to explore my vocation would have been missed, and I am forever grateful to him for that. By his example, he showed that he meant me no harm and only sought my greatest good. On July 16, 1977, he died suddenly as a result of a brain disease, just like my father.

MORE THAN A BOSS

It took three months as a student teacher in a Catholic secondary modern school learning to educate eleven- to fifteen-year-old boys and girls in a suburb of Birmingham, to realize it was not the career for me. The preparation and presentation of material were enjoyable, but to maintain discipline and order, I had to act out the role of being a strict, no-nonsense teacher rather than do something that was naturally comfortable. St. Joseph's school in Nechells moved its senior pupils to its new location in Leigh Road, Washwood Heath in 1963, and teachers and pupils alike were adjusting to the move when I joined them for the summer term of 1965.

It took two years and three months as an articled clerk with a firm of chartered accountants in the city of Birmingham to realize that confirming that profit and loss and balance sheets represented a true and fair statement of the trading operations, assets and liabilities of a company was not the career for me either. Certainly, I found the business world to be exciting and very challenging, but what attracted me more was the human side of the enterprise. Whenever we, as a team of auditors, visited clients, I took every opportunity to escape from reconciling bank or ledger accounts or from verifying inventories to pay a visit to the personnel department to talk about people issues. Topics ranged from employee relations to recruitment, selection, development, training and termination.

A year after joining the firm of accountants, I was becoming restless. In 1966, a friend wanted me to go with him to South Africa after the World Cup football (soccer) tournament, which, surprisingly, England won. In September of that same year, I seriously considered returning to the academic world to study psychology. The Joint Matriculation Board covering the universities of Manchester, Liverpool, Leeds Sheffield and Birmingham accepted my application to study at any of their establishments. However, it, along with the thought of emigrating, conflicted with a former decision I had made to repay my parents for the financial sacrifices they had made for me to study for the priesthood, so I discontinued pursuing those paths for the time being. The partners at the firm persuaded me to complete my intermediate examinations that were to be held in the summer of 1967 before deciding what to do with my career.

Although in the worlds of fashion and pop music England was experiencing the "swinging sixties" with miniskirts turning heads and with The Beatles, The Rolling Stones, The Kinks and The Who making people stamp their feet, problems were brewing elsewhere in the economy. The ailing vehicle manufacturing industry was in desperate need of reorganization. There were too many car models, many only built with right-hand drive, which limited markets to the UK and a few other countries worldwide. There were too many small manufacturing sites supplying parts to assembly plants. In addition, the relations between management and unions were at an all-time low, as both sides were constantly arguing about antiquated piecework payments. Wildcat strikes were on the increase, and the ability to forecast the future was becoming impossible for company boards of directors.

The more I read the newspaper headlines, the more I wanted to become part of the solution. After completing my intermediate Chartered Accountant examinations, I applied in autumn 1967 for a position in the personnel department of the Rover Company in the neighboring town of Solihull. Rover was an established company that produced luxury cars mainly for the UK market and Land Rover four-wheel drive vehicles that had been selling well internationally. In addition, Rover had been in the forefront of research and development of a gas turbine engine based on the principles of the turbojet engine invented by Sir Frank Whittle.

I recall vividly driving down the main entrance of the Rover Company at Lode Lane Solihull. It was a hive of activity with lines of trucks, vans and passenger cars checking in and out of the security gates. An impressive modern research and development building dominated the view on the left side of the road. Given a sticker, I proceeded to the visitor's car park on the right side of the road in front of the stately administrative offices. Not only was there a constant flow of vehicles, but there was a constant flow of people, some in suits, some in overalls, some in white coats and many dressed in skirts. The scene reminded me of one of Lowry's matchstick people paintings that had suddenly come to life. I followed the procession making its way to the personnel block. It was particularly lively, as production was being increased and people were applying for jobs as assembly workers.

Following a series of preliminary interviews, I was ushered into the office of Mr. Richards, who introduced himself to me as Ted, the director of personnel. He made it clear that the industry was facing major challenges and a turbulent future with a requirement for tremendous change. In 1967, Leyland Motors, which owned Triumph Cars, had just taken over Rover, and that was only the beginning. In the final analysis, I was offered a job as a staff job analyst or evaluation officer responsible for studying clerical, supervisory, technical and middle management positions so that they could be properly graded and slotted into the correct salary ranges. The total number of staff was approximately 3,000 in number, spread over several locations. This work would support the teams responsible for staff recruitment and selection and staff union relations, particularly the latter, as they were constantly negotiating with officials of trade unions who wanted to increase the salaries of their members. In the first few months, the workload was heavy and the learning curve steep, but it totally engrossed me, so much so that I enrolled in what is now Aston University to study to gain professional qualifications in personnel management. Ted Richards was correct, change was on its way.

Almost a year later, a new office was opened next to the one in which our team of three worked. We were introduced to its new occupant, Hugh Austin. He had been heavily involved in the human and administrative side of the gas turbine engine development project pioneered by the brilliant engineer Spencer "Spen" King. This project was considered by many as the most advanced work undertaken by any car manufacturer. Success had been achieved in France at the

1963 Le Mans twenty-four-hour race. However, the project was brought to an abrupt end, and the managing director of Rover Group asked Hugh to join the personnel department. His prime responsibility was to improve company leadership by unlocking homegrown potential and recruiting a higher caliber of managerial staff and management trainees. He was given a budget for a management development assistant to help him in this important task.

Although he was sixteen years my senior, Hugh was a very friendly, very modest and approachable person. He did not restrict our conversations to the future needs of Rover or, indeed, its history, but showed an interest in talking about personal matters, our lives and dreams. He told me about his time at Lincoln College, Oxford, where he studied history, and how impressed he was with a fellow history student, Peter Parker, who went on to become Sir Peter Parker, the charismatic Chairman of British Rail under Margaret Thatcher. His studies in history were interrupted by the Second World War. He joined the Royal Navy and became an officer on several minesweepers. He also spent some time with the Coastal Forces in command of a motor torpedo boat (MTB). As I had often visited the docks in Liverpool and seen many of the biggest ocean liners moored in the river Mersey, we had a mutual interest in the sea. My uncle Joe was a merchant seaman who used to visit my aunt Ellen and tell us tales of his adventures. History was also an interest we shared, especially local history. After the war, Hugh returned to Oxford to complete his studies and gain his degree.

Apart from the sea and English history, we had many other things in common. He lived in Norton Lindsey, a village not far from the town of Warwick, which I knew well. My first year of study for the priesthood was spent at a stately home in Hampton-on-the-Hill, called Grove Park, which belonged to the Lord Dormer estate.

The grounds had been landscaped by the famous architect Capability Brown, and the lake was a favorite venue of mine. I used to go there to reflect on the ideas being disseminated during our philosophy sessions. Often when running, I would pass through Norton Lindsey, never imagining I would get to know one of its residents.

When I first met Hugh in 1968, he had been married for two years to Marion. He was forty years old when he tied the knot but was excited by the prospect of raising a family. Many weekends he would travel south to spend time with his elderly mother and also exercise his sailing skills. He was so unassuming that I was surprised to learn that he was involved in many ocean races, had sailed across the Atlantic and was a founder member of the Ocean Cruising Club. In one of the Club's publications, a reference is made to him: "These two transatlantic races, 1950 and 1952, supplied a total of 15 Founder Members... and Hugh Austin who raced in *Joliette*." He is also included in the lists of the Founder Members, and there is a record of his trip from Bermuda-Plymouth where a total of 2,850 miles is registered.

In the workplace, Hugh advertised for a graduate with experience in the relatively new field of management development to become his assistant. Over the following weeks, we saw a number of candidates go through the interview process. Out of curiosity, I asked Hugh's secretary to let me know when an offer was made. One afternoon, Hugh called me into his office and told me he had interviewed all internal and external candidates. He informed me that no one had met his requirements precisely and asked me whether I would be interested in being considered for the position. To put it mildly, I was flabbergasted and gratefully accepted the opportunity. After being formally interviewed, he called me into his office and offered me the job. Dumbstruck, I sat with bated breath and could not believe my good fortune. All I could say was, "Thank you. Thank you. Thank you. You won't regret it."

Hugh Austin on his wedding day in 1966

By inviting me to join his think tank, Hugh encouraged me to not only study best practice, but to also study what could be the next practice. We needed to come up with practical proposals to improve all levels of management and prepare a pipeline of people with managerial potential. I accompanied him to meetings with senior managers and learned so much about how to conduct myself and focus on their understanding and real needs. At appropriate times, he would invite my contributions on a subject he knew I had researched. When he felt confident, he let me loose to venture forth on my own. Afterward, we would review such sessions and he would suggest certain areas that could be explored on future occasions. I learned much by studying his correspondence, as he had a very good turn of phrase, was succinct but clear, complimentary without being deferential.

Hugh broadened my mind by sending me to London to keep up to date with new ideas coming from the United States, such as management by objectives. He gave me books like *The Effective Executive* by Peter Drucker for study and discussion. He arranged for me to be taught to interview by psychologists at the National Institute of Industrial Psychology (NIIP), where I became proficient in the use of the "Seven-Point Plan" devised by Sir Alec Rodger for employment selection purposes. This structured approach was first published in 1955 after research that began in 1930. Interestingly, one of the professors at Aston University, Munro Frazer, had developed a similar five-point plan. Selection interviewing became a major interest of mine that continues to this day. I believe that there has to be a combination of structure and openness that reveals a person's strengths and weaknesses with optimum accuracy.

Hugh was a meticulous planner, and I learned much from him when it came to arranging the graduate recruitment and selection program. We were responsible for candidates not only for Rover Triumph, but also for Jaguar. We used group assessment methods over a two-day period at a local hotel. Everything went like clockwork for both graduates and the management involved in their selection. We introduced a management appraisal system that measured as objectively as possible each manager's performance and potential. We also compiled attendant succession plans in collaboration with senior management. Although I only worked with Hugh for two and a half years, my growth as a personnel professional and also as a person was exponential. I had grown in self-confidence and felt comfortable mingling with all levels of employees. The advice given and ideas exchanged were to prove a strong foundation upon which to move forward. It was not long before Hugh and I were affected by inevitable organizational changes.

A decision was made to integrate Rover and Triumph and gain the economic benefits of such a merger. A small team was set up in March 1971 for this purpose, and I was chosen to become an organization planning analyst for commercial operations. What I had learned from Hugh served me well in this role, which would open further doors. Indeed, my time working with Hugh was critical in my development. Many seeds were planted in my mind to flourish later. The assessment centers developed for graduate selection enabled me to participate in and create assessment centers that were developed to select superintendents in the seventies at Austin Rover, and, in the eighties, we used development centers to detail career plans for high flyers with great leadership potential. Another lesson learned from Hugh was the importance of being a lifelong learner dedicated to continuous self-improvement. I took every opportunity to learn about selection methods and in the seventies became qualified to administer and interpret aptitude tests and personality questionnaires and studied the measurement of human factors, or psychometrics. In the early eighties, the work of Maurice Belbin absorbed my interest, as he developed methods to identify team roles that best suited team members and contributed to successful teams. Hugh stimulated my interest in structured interviews, and I studied behavioral-based and situational interviews, or combinations of them, together with biographical interviews to select people. As a result of these active interests, I started to study psychology and joined the British Psychological Society (BPS).

When working in Tokyo in 1989, rumors were circulating that Rover Cars was going to be sold and Honda and BMW were speculated to be potential buyers. There were fears that BMW was keen to add the Mini car to its range of models and wanted the brand. I had taken models of the Mini car with me to celebrate the production of the millionth Mini at Longbridge that year. BMW was not only interested in the Mini, but also in the technology behind the Range Rover. On return from Tokyo, I came to the conclusion that Rover Cars was destined to die soon, assets would be stripped and the whole operation dismantled. There and then, I decided to change careers and become a full-time occupational psychologist working in the business world, and I began reviewing opportunities. Prior to leaving Rover Cars at the end of June 1991, I had completed all my formal studies in psychology and just required experience before I could be upgraded to the level of associate fellow of the BPS.

Another thing Hugh and I had in common was a dry or deadpan sense of humor. Often, we would sit and laugh at items that had been found on management appraisal reports. For instance:

"This man is always in the right place at the right time, well out of sight!"

"This man catches a train of thought, usually via the guard's van."

"Some people create happiness wherever they go, but Jones creates happiness whenever he goes!"

"Did this person get a Ph.D. in upsetting people, or does it come naturally to him?"

Although Hugh's career progressed along a different trajectory, I would often call him for advice, and our paths crossed from time to time. We were always pleased to see each other and connected and engaged just like in the old days in the offices at Solihull. Hugh never took himself too seriously. It is interesting to me that his penultimate job before he retired was running the personnel department of Freight Rover based in Common Lane, Birmingham, a mere stone's throw away from the secondary modern school of St. Joseph's, where I started my career as a student teacher. Following further reorganization, Hugh transferred to Leyland DAF to complete his career in the human resources function in the automotive industry.

Hugh was a very proud and devoted husband and father to Sarah and twins Geoff and Rachel and a true friend to me. Whenever I think of Hugh, the proverb "silent waters run deep" comes to mind. We kept in touch through cards and occasional correspondence until he died on March 8, 2012. When Maureen and I went to the UK in 2013 to celebrate Maureen's seventieth birthday and our daughter, Larissa's, thirty-ninth birthday, we spent some quality time with Marion reminiscing and sharing anecdotes and insights into Hugh's life, a life well lived. I am grateful to Hugh for the opportunity he gave me to work as his assistant and learn from him. Most bosses focus mainly on the work at hand, but Hugh was more than a boss, as he took a personal interest in me and my broader career, hopes and aspirations. He truly was a mentor who meant me no harm and sought my greatest good.

MORE THAN A PSYCHOLOGIST

Separated by thirty-four years and over 3,500 miles, when we first met, Dr. William E. Hall and I quickly realized we were on the same wavelength. We were both interested in the power of human relationships and the interplay between thoughts and feelings and their expression in behavior. We were both intrigued by the power of structured interviews to help identify human potential, which we were keen to unlock. We first met in the spring of 1991 at his office in Atlanta, Georgia in the United States. The meeting was the final stage in a long recruitment and selection process that began at the beginning of the previous year. At that time, I was actively looking for an opportunity to work as a business psychologist and had one or two exploratory discussions with headhunting firms in the UK because of my deep interest in interviewing methods and assessment techniques that involved the use of psychological tests, various forms of structured interviews and group exercises.

On return from a European business trip in February 1990 while sorting my mail, I picked up the latest copy of a periodical from the British Psychological Society (BPS) and pulled out an insert called the BPS Memorandum of Appointments in which current vacancies were displayed. The majority of advertisements were trying to attract the attention of clinical psychologists. The main focus of recruiters was on the treatment of people who were in some way failing to cope or to some degree broken. It seemed to me at the time that their adverts were looking for psychologists who were experts in failure. After wading through page after page of such adverts, one particular advertisement placed by a company called Talent Plus ® stood out. It asked four evocative questions that I could answer in the affirmative and gained my immediate attention and interest:

- Are you empathetic, decisive and do you have the courage of your convictions?
- Are you intrigued with becoming a 'student' of successful individuals throughout the world?
- Do you want to write, see results for your efforts, meet deadlines and ultimately become a 'people consultant' dedicated to serving clients all over the United Kingdom, United States and Canada?
- Are you interested in a tremendous opportunity to associate with a quality consulting firm and a chance to learn from people considered 'the best' by a variety of industries?

Candidates were asked to send their CV to Dr. William E. Hall through an adviser based in Coventry, United Kingdom. This opportunity seemed to be just up my street, so a copy of my résumé and a covering letter were dispatched without delay. Shortly afterwards, I was contacted by a lady with an American accent who introduced herself as Sandy Maxwell, calling from Talent Plus, to set up an interview, which she stated would take approximately two hours. Assuming the interview was to be held in the United States, I mentioned that my travel plans to eight of the National Sales Companies of Rover Cars had been set in concrete for March, April and early May, so it was going to be difficult to travel to the United States during that timeframe. She explained that the interview would be conducted over the telephone, so at this stage travel arrangements were not necessary. A date of May 17, 1990, was fixed and the time set was in the early evening Greenwich Mean Time.

At that time, I was researching the predictive validity and reliability of selection interviews and was not at all familiar with or had experience of being interviewed by a person whose body language was not available for interpretation. I knew the tone of voice expressed emotional states pretty well, but in the absence of other physical features, it was difficult to interpret. This was an experience I was looking forward to and one which I could research further in my studies on the effectiveness of selection and development interviews.

I was not disappointed; the interview was very thought provoking and contained biographical questions and behavioral-based questions. There were also questions that explored the handling of situations I had never experienced. There were questions relating to personality, intellectual acumen, people acumen, motives, interests, intentions and levels of drive. Most of the questions could be interpreted and answered in several different ways, and it was left up to me to decide how best to respond. There were no time limits or restrictions. I was allowed at any time to clarify something said previously by adding to or changing my response. It was a fascinating experience and I could not wait to see how effectively I had answered the questions. I remember thinking that it would be great to meet the brains behind the questions.

Shortly after the interview, arrangements were made for me to meet the chairman of Talent Plus, Doug Rath, who was visiting the United Kingdom. We dined in a famous seafood restaurant in Kensington, London, and he whetted my appetite as far as his vision for the company was concerned. We kept in touch and next met in Harrogate, shortly after his discussions with the leaders of Greenalls Brewery Limited, which wanted to use Talent Plus as a human resources consultancy. In a public house in Yorkshire during a snow blizzard in January 1991, we agreed that I would fly to Lincoln, Nebraska, to meet the other founders of Talent Plus, Kimberly Rath and Sandy Maxwell, and then travel to Atlanta, Georgia to meet Dr. Hall, followed by a visit to Winchester, Virginia to meet Bill Brandt, who had provided some money to launch the company.

It is interesting to consider that in September 1989, after concluding that I would leave Rover Cars during my visit to Tokyo, I had taken a flight to San Francisco where I spent a few days relaxing before flying from Oakland Airport to Chicago on my way to Miami to visit the National Sales Company for Rover Cars in the United States. As we flew over the Rockies, the pilot pointed out Denver, the Mile High City, and mentioned that we would cross the plains en route to Chicago. As I peered out of the window and scanned a patchwork of squares and circles that made up the landscape, it never entered my mind – indeed, it was totally out of the question – that I would ultimately end up working in

Lincoln, the state capital of Nebraska, in a company that was registered there three months earlier in July 1989.

It was now the end of March, 1991, as the plane taxied along the long runway to the jet way and the beginning of a life-changing whirlwind tour. Doug took me to the Talent Plus offices, which were located on the second floor in an office block on 48th Street, Lincoln, next to a sign marked *Amigos*. Certainly, the people inside were very friendly, although the offices were quite poky. There I met and spent time with Kimberly, Doug's wife, Sandy Maxwell and the young man who interviewed me over the telephone, Andrew Bartek. It was difficult not to like them, as they made such a fuss, treated me as one of the family and wanted to know all about me and my family and find out what England was like, even though Doug and Kimberly were quite frequent visitors to the United Kingdom.

The next day, Doug and I flew to Atlanta, Georgia, to meet Dr. Bill Hall and his wife, Susan. Due to weather conditions, we had to go via St. Louis, which allowed Doug to give me a brief history of Dr. Hall and his connection with Talent Plus, where he held the title of vice chairman. Doug told me that Dr. Hall had been the professor of educational psychology and measurement at the University of Nebraska-Lincoln (UNL) between 1945 and 1969, during which time he had founded the Nebraska Human Resources Foundation (NHRF) to help student teachers mentor high school pupils with potential. In 1969, Dr. Hall resigned from the University of Nebraska and along with Dr. Don Clifton, a work colleague and one of his former Ph.D. students, founded Selection Research Inc. (SRI). Doug and Kimberly had been members of NHRF and employees of SRI, which bought Gallup in 1988. In 1974, Dr. Hall resigned from SRI and set up his own consultancy, Hall Research Institute, before moving to Atlanta in 1976 to be near his eldest daughter, Dorothy. There he established a new company, Psychological Selection Inc., with Susan. Doug and Kimberly left Gallup in March 1989 and reconnected with Dr. Hall to set up Talent Plus in July of that year and had been growing the business slowly since then. Doug also told me that Dr. Hall was a student of Dr. Carl Rogers, arguably the most influential American psychologist of the 20th century, and that Dr. Hall was a pioneer of both positive psychology and structured interviews within the United States. Finally, he mentioned that Bill had recently had two angioplasties to improve his blood circulation and that although he was eighty-three years old, he was still highly productive.

It was with some trepidation that I entered his suite of offices, where Susan Hall greeted us and ushered us in to meet her husband. Dr. Hall was tall and thin and quite frail, but he beamed like a lighthouse and had a positive glint in his eyes, which seemed totally focused on me. After the usual pleasantries, we got down to the interview, which consisted of one polite instruction from by Dr. Hall, "Please tell me what you know about empathy."

This had been my favorite area of study, and I had read everything I could get hold of about empathy and had even written a poem on the subject. Animated, I explained my ideas about rational empathy, emotional empathy and how they differed from sympathy, et cetera, et cetera. When I finally finished, he leaned over to me and stated, "When you come to work with me, you'll learn a lot more about empathy!"

Dr. Bill Hall, 1963. Love library archives, UNL

He then turned to Doug and asked, "Is Jim coming to live in the United States?

Doug started laughing, as Dr. Hall was jumping the gun somewhat.

After leaving Atlanta, I went to Winchester, Virginia, as planned, to meet Bill Brandt, the chairman of American Woodmark, a kitchen cabinet manufacturing business. I assumed he was also going to pass judgment on me. Following discussions with Bill Brandt, I returned to England with the refrain, "When you come to work with me, you'll learn a lot more about empathy" ringing in my ears.

Dr. Hall was a very wise and humble man who had a wealth of knowledge and was an accomplished teacher from whom much could be learned. I decided on my flight home, if given an offer to work with him, I would accept it. For many years, I had been working in an industry that was declining. It would be a change and a challenge to help a company grow. During my twenty-three years and eight months with Rover Cars, I had worked with many brilliant professionals and had been instrumental in the growth and success of many talented performers and leaders, which was something I wanted to do with a new company that had a new outlook. When I told Maureen and Larissa, they thought I was crazy and going through a version of the male menopause. They told me that they could not accompany me, as Maureen was a committed teacher and Larissa was just about to start her sixth form, or senior high school studies.

An offer came in May, 1991. It was very different to the offers I had been making to potential employees of Rover Cars, which tended to be four or five pages in length and emphasized the employment contract. Such offers focused on the need for parties to understand the legal terms and conditions. Employment contracts were basically economic contracts that outlined salary and benefits in exchange for work carried out. When I opened the envelope from Talent Plus, it contained a one-page offer and a five-page profile assessing my strengths, which was written by Dr. Hall. The profile ended by Dr. Hall stating, "We would not be writing this evaluation if we did not think Talent Plus was offering Mr. Meehan the most significant match of a career opportunity with his talent. We believe he cannot afford to disregard this opportunity on any basis." It seemed to me that the focus of the Talent Plus selection process was the psychological contract. It focused on mutual beliefs, values and mutual obligations. The emphasis was on strengths rather than ensuring that the candidate had no serious weaknesses, and on the development of potential rather than remediation of gaps of knowledge, skills or experience. I had been searching for something I would love to do, people with whom I would like to work, the freedom to become better and have my life and work more fully integrated. Now I had found it.

So I left Rover Cars at the end of June 1991, and made arrangements to join Dr. Hall on the first of August in Atlanta. To show Maureen and Larissa that I would be in safe hands, I took them on a trip that spanned Lincoln, Nebraska; Disney World in Orlando, Florida; and Atlanta, Georgia, to meet all the members of Talent Plus. Maureen and Larissa were convinced that I had made the right decision and wished me well. After we parted at Hartsfield Airport on July 31, a new and exciting phase in my life was about to begin – my friendship with Dr. Hall, who became my mentor. I have written a book about the lessons learned from Dr. Hall called *Hall Ways to Success and Significance: The Positive Force of Dr. William E. Hall.* This is linked to a website that contains a copy of a scrapbook I compiled about him called "A Life Spent Creating Something Which Outlived It." These works provide a fuller account of Bill, the man and the influence he had not only on me, but on countless others, whose lives he turned upside down or, as I prefer to put it, the right way up. While professionally Bill was a brilliant teacher, coach and trainer, what made him my mentor was his interest in me as a person and in the broader goals and aspirations I had for my life and his willingness to help me and befriend me. Just like my other mentors, he told me stories about his life and lessons he had learned and the things he had yet to achieve. When I spent time with him, he gave me total positive regard and, by revealing the best in himself, brought out the best in me.

Dr. Hall, who asked me to call him Bill, told me that he was born in McGregor, Iowa, on August 19, 1907, the son of a Methodist preacher. He was one of six children. He recalled being able to read by the age of four and being part of a very musical family. His father's ministry involved much travel, and he told me about his schooldays in Montana and Idaho, where he attended high school at La Payette in Boise, Idaho. From high school, he went to Idaho College in Caldwell before moving to Willamette University in Salem, Oregon, to study political science. There he met his wife to be, Susan, and married her on September 17, 1930. He graduated in 1932, and, as there was no work available due to the Great Depression, he and Susan went to La Grande Normal School in Oregon, where he gained his teaching certificate in 1933.

Next, they moved to Pleasant Valley, Oregon, where they taught in a one-classroom school for a while before Bill obtained a role as the principal of an elementary school in Eagle Valley in the neighboring town of Richland, Oregon. Bill became fascinated by gifted children and their potential and decided in 1939 to go with his wife and two children, Vernon and Dorothy, to Ohio State University in Columbus, Ohio, to study psychology. In 1940, he gained his master's degree and stayed on to complete the formal studies that contributed to his doctoral program. He told me about his attendance at the lectures of Dr. Carl Rogers, with whom he personally did not particularly get along, but from whom he learned a great deal. Dr. Rogers provided him with a reference to become an assistant professor at Eastern Washington College in Cheney, Washington State, where he completed his thesis. In December, 1943, he was awarded his Ph.D. from Ohio State University.

In 1945, as Doug had mentioned, Dr. Hall and his family moved to Lincoln, where he completed his family with the additions of Louise and John. The NHRF, which he founded in 1949, was renamed the Nebraska Human Resources Institute (NHRI) in 1988 and it continues to this day to develop leaders for Nebraska and the nation.

What Bill achieved during his lifetime was quite remarkable. He was one of the pioneers of positive psychology. He was the father of success and strength psychology and of totally structured selection interviews. His structured interviews not only had set questions but also had set conceptual matches to which candidates' responses could be compared. In addition, his interviews were allowed to be totally open ended and as stress minimum as possible. His Foundation is 65 years old and Talent Plus is currently experiencing its 25-year anniversary. After Bill died, I was honored to be asked to give a eulogy at his funeral. Subsequently, I visited his high school and all the colleges and universities where he studied or taught and searched the archives. In addition, I read everything I could find, not only material that he wrote about his work but also everything others have written about his life and work. As a result of my experience and analysis, it became evident to me that through his life and work, Bill invited people to become successful and significant. While Bill recognized that success could be seen in terms of personal achievements, from the point of view of professional roles, he insisted in using as many measures as possible of the performance in question. To Bill, significance was inexorably linked with doing something worthwhile, something that matters or adds value to people. I started grouping his main ideas under headings, namely relationships, strengths, vision, values, virtue and positivity.

One evening while browsing my notes, I noticed that the first letters of the categories, RSVP, were the letters found at the bottom of invitations to feasts and funerals. The acronym R.S.V.P. summarizes the French expression, "Respondez s'il vous plait," which translates into "Please reply."

"Wow!" I thought, "That makes sense. The perfect response to Bill's invitation is to adopt his ways."

The acronym stands for:

Building good relationships – R
Investing in strengths – S
Being vision, value and virtue driven – V
Adopting a positive approach – P

Some people see life as a sprint, others see life as marathon. I support those who see life as a relay race. Bill passed a baton to me, and it is my privilege to hand the baton to others. Accordingly, one of my key responsibilities is to help people to respond to Bill's invitation to achieve success and significance by not only giving their R.S.V.P., but by living it, too! The response IS the way to go. Although the book *Hall Ways to Success and Significance* contains a detailed professional personal history and provides a chapter on each of his ways, plus copious references to his writing and works and testimonies about his work, I thought it would be useful to provide some insights and calls for action resulting from his research.

RELATIONSHIPS

For Bill, successful and significant people build good relationships with others. His definition of a good or desirable relationship is one that benefits all parties in the relationship. As I put it, good relationships build and bad relationships break. Bill never underestimated the power of relationships to bring out the best in people. He realized that the best way to help somebody grow is to have a good relationship with him or her. This should not be so surprising when we consider that almost every person comes into this world as a result of a relationship between their mum and dad. Moreover, the human potential each baby has when it is born, that is, its natural endowment, is going to be unlocked and brought to full bloom by the relationships the baby will have throughout its life, with its caregivers, its teachers, its pastors, its professors, its mentors, its lovers, its close friends, its supporters and obviously with itself.

Bill invested in relationships as intensely as financial brokers invest in shares on the stock exchange. His science was the science of people at their best, at their strongest and people at their most noble. Indeed, he promoted what he called "investment relationships" to improve individuals, groups and society as a whole. He realized that when person A invests in person B, for person B's sake, there is always a hidden return that helps A to grow. It is as though we were all connected, all in some sense, one entity. As mentioned earlier, psychological researchers have discovered that in many cases mentors grow more than their protégés. In addition, Bill found that in an investment relationship, person A helps person B to invest in others, which, in turn, helps B to grow. A chain reaction is set in motion, which Dr. Hall called the "ripple effect." His research at UNL and the operation of his Foundation showed that he achieved his best results when his best counselors were matched with the best high school students. Equally he found in the workplace the best results were achieved when top performers mentored or coached the best upcoming performers. Dr. Hall's experiments with investment relationships emphasized the connectedness of people to each other. By helping you, I am in reality helping myself!

The idea of everyone being connected or in some sense being one has a long history. In philosophy, it goes back to Zeno of Citium, a town on the southern shores of Cyprus. When he moved to Athens, Zeno taught philosophy under the *Stoa Poikile*, 'the painted colonnade' on the north side of the ancient agora of Athens – hence the name, 'Stoic.' The Stoics held that the universe was one and that there was a master plan, and everything was happening for a reason. The ancient Greeks saw self-knowledge as a key to wisdom. "Know thyself," was one of three inscriptions on the sun god Apollo's Oracle of Delphi temple. I think many of the

Greek philosophers learned about themselves not only by self-reflection but also through the feedback they received from others. In religious circles, Buddhists see the universe as one entity. In the world of psychology, Carl Gustav Jung declared that all humans were connected by a 'collective unconscious.' Recently I read two books about near-death experiences, both on the U.S. best sellers list: *Dying to be Me*, by Anita Moorjani and *Proof of Heaven* by Eben Alexander, M.D. Both had been declared to all intents and purposes dead. They both experienced comas, which were followed by what can only be described as miraculous recoveries, Moorjani from a very aggressive form of cancer and Alexander from a rare brain disease.

When Moorjani entered into her near-death state, she described her initial insight as follows: *"I became aware that we're all connected.* This was not only every person and living creature, but the interwoven unification felt as though it were expanding outward to include everything in the universe – every human, animal, plant, insect, mountain, sea, inanimate object, and the cosmos. I realized that the entire universe is alive and infused with consciousness, encompassing all of life and nature. Everything belongs to an infinite Whole. I was intricately, inseparably enmeshed with all of life. We're all One, each of us has an effect on the collective Whole."

Alexander, himself a neuroscientist, in his near-death experience went on a journey and explained, "What I discovered out beyond is the indescribable immensity and complexity of the universe, and that consciousness is the basis of all that exists. I was so totally connected to it that there was often no real differentiation between "me" and the world I was moving through... We – each of us – are intricately, irremovably connected to a larger universe."

Relationships never stand still; they either grow or die. Bill urged people to not let a day go by without auditing their key relationships. For me, a simple way of doing this is first to consider whether we give important people in our lives adequate attention, adequate time and listen to them adequately enough. Second, we need to draw up an action plan to deal with any inadequacies. We could even take it two steps further by meeting the people in question one on one and asking them if they thought that we gave them adequate attention, adequate time, and gave them an adequate listening ear and discuss how we can further improve our relationship. Everyone needs this fundamental form of recognition but has to have it tailored to their individual needs. Top performers and mediocre ones both need it. Bill thought that top performers were often taken for granted and the opportunity to accelerate their growth was not seized. I know from conducting exit interviews with leaders that in many cases, they leave companies and go elsewhere hoping to receive a more adequate degree of attention and time and be listened to more.

Accordingly, when asked by people about how best to develop and maintain good relationships, I ask them to use an acronym, ATL. It stands for attention, time and listening. To help them remember the acronym, I often write on a flip-chart or pronounce another well-used acronym, ATM, and ask them what it stands for. They quickly let me know that "automatic telling machine" is the full version. I then ask them whether money can buy them love. They usually agree with The Beatles who wrote a song called "Money Can't Buy Me Love." So I reinforce the point that for good relationships, think ATL not ATM!

For Bill, ignorance was never bliss when it came to establishing good relationships. He placed the highest priority on identifying people whom he could trust and had what he called credibility, that is, the power to inspire confidence. In good relationships, he was also aware that people need to feel that they are trusted as well. Bill believed that crises of trust need to be addressed, two people at a time. While his theories about building good relationships expanded my mind, he also provided me with actual experiences that reinforced his views.

After a couple of weeks working with Bill, I was in the outer office talking to Susan, who acted as his assistant, when all of a sudden we heard a crash in his office. When we ran in, Bill was stretched out on the floor, lying on his back, white as a sheet and out cold. He was still breathing, but we called for paramedics, who arrived and took Bill and Susan to the local hospital. I was left to look after the fort. I informed Sandy Maxwell in the corporate office in Lincoln, then sat and reflected. Fine mess I was in! Having left a good job with really exceptional benefits to learn from a guru, I was now afraid that it could all come to an abrupt end. Fortunately, Bill was just dehydrated and simply needed to drink more water. One lesson I learned was the fragility of health. This spurred me to learn as much as I could during my time with Bill. Another more important lesson followed over the next month or so.

Something strange was beginning to happen. People kept on coming up to me to ask what I was doing to Bill.

"Hold on a minute, don't you mean what is Bill doing to me?" I protested. "He is totally changing my perspective! So precisely what are you talking about?"

They told me that since Bill had begun working with me, color had returned to his cheeks, he was walking more upright, there was more of a bounce in his step and he was generally more exuberant. On further consideration, I realized that the mentoring relationship was bringing out the best in us, that is, actualizing our potential more fully. He was being changed physically and I was being changed mentally. Yes, I had read about the transformational power of relationships, but that was all theoretical and at times semantic. Now I was in the process of experiencing the benefits derived from a good relationship. I began reflecting on other relationships in my life and noticed how deeply they had changed the parties involved. Even when people die, we often ask, "What would X have done in this situation?" We allow our memories of them to affect us. I suddenly realized the power of human relationships to help people become more fully alive not just mentally, but physically. Moreover, that experience was very deep.

Dr. Hall promised that when I came to work with him I would learn more about empathy. He certainly delivered on that promise. Not so long ago, I found myself in a similar situation to Bill when he interviewed me. I was talking to two psychology graduates from UNL about the meaning of empathy. They appeared to have reached the same conclusions I embraced just before meeting Dr. Hall. As the discussion was drawing to a close and I had another meeting to attend, I summarized by stating that their position was that there were two forms of empathy, rational and emotional and that the former could be expressed by the statement, "I understand what you're going through," and the latter by the sentence " I feel your pain." They agreed.

I then asked, "Would you be surprised if I were to tell you that those conclusions were not total empathy?"

"You bet!" they replied.

So I said, "Prepare to be surprised, as your position does not capture the full meaning of total empathy." Adopting the style of Dr. Hall, I asked them to think it over and we would meet again later to discuss the subject further.

Several weeks later, we met and they told me that they had reviewed their position and talked it over with their tutors and respectfully rejected my contention. I asked them to tell me what they heard when I repeated the two expressions "I understand what you're going through. I feel your pain." They found them to be a succinct definition of true empathy. I explained that above all else, for me, empathy was a relationship between two people. The expressions seemed to me to place the emphasis on the "I," and not so much on the "other." The statements were too egocentric for my liking.

"It is more about ME, capital M, capital E," I stressed. "Empathy does not really become empathy until the other person knows that you truly understand what they are going through and that you do indeed feel what they are feeling," I continued. "The best way to convey this to the other person is to take some action to help him or her. On occasion, active listening may be the only adequate response that can be made. Active listening engages the other person in a way that merely hearing what they say does not. Genuine emotions can be conveyed in many open ways like hugging and in subtle ways by using appropriate facial expressions. Total empathy is an active two-way process. One-way empathy is like unrequited love. I can be deeply in love with someone, but if I never tell the other person or fail to take actions to express my thoughts and feelings, it will remain personal. Is it love? Yes, it is. But it still falls short of what is meant by a total loving relationship," I concluded.

We discussed the matter at some length and decided that there was a need to ensure that a balance between "I" and "other" needed to be found in any final definition of total empathy. We also agreed that just as 'tough love' needs to be exercised at times, we also need to give people 'tough empathy,' which means meeting their real needs, not necessarily giving them just what they want.

It can be helpful from time to time to make a list of people who have been highly influential in our lives on a personal or professional basis and note the ways they continue to impact us, and then letting them know, especially if we feel that they may not be aware. Even if we feel they know it, telling them again will foster or renew our relationship. Carrying out this exercise helps to avoid 'one-way' streaks in our relationships and ensures mutual awareness and reciprocity exist. Unrequited or unfulfilled relationships can thereby be avoided.

Dr. Hall used what he called his 'in-depth structured interviews' to see whether he could trust an individual and to examine his or her credibility. Prior to founding Talent Plus, all the interviews he conducted were carried out face to face and recorded and not conducted over the telephone, which is how the majority of Talent Plus interviews are executed nowadays.

While he was at UNL, Bill experimented with a relationship-building tool that became known as "Focus On You ®." He used it to demonstrate that spending a short amount of time focusing on each person in a group at the outset facilitates the process of building good human relationships. Bill insisted that people need to make an effort to get to know others because it does not always come about naturally. In summary, it is a structured method of allowing each person in a group to answer a few set questions about aspects of their personal and professional interests, successes and goals. Although it was initially used as an ice breaker and was designed to accentuate the positives, it has become a very flexible tool that can explore areas in which individuals feel they would benefit from a certain amount of help. It can also be used in one-on-one sessions during the exploratory stages of a relationship. More details of this tool can be found in *Hall Ways to Success and Significance.*

See *References* (pp.185-186) for details of two interesting studies, one on empathy as being an angry and affective response (Professor Robert Bringle et al.) and the other examining the difference between empathy and sympathy (Katy Davis and Dr. Brené Brown).

STRENGTHS

For Bill, successful and significant people invest in their own strengths and in the strengths of others. He regarded human strengths to be inexorably linked to human relationships. I never found a precise definition of a strength in Bill's works. He appeared to take its meaning for granted. My analysis of his writings and our conversations convinced me that a strength has two components. First, it is something a person does well or has the potential to do well. In other words, it is a talent. Second, it is something which the person is really passionate about or truly enjoys. A strength is a talent on steroids! While every strength is a talent, not every talent is a strength. Talent is necessary but not sufficient. Just because a person enjoys exercising a strength does not mean that it is always easy. Getting to the top of a mountain or running a full marathon are hard but, when completed, very satisfying or enjoyable in the sense of accomplishment. The good news is that every time we invest in strengths and use them properly, we grow. They are gifts that keep on giving. Eloquence can be a strength when presenting, but, when counseling, if a person talks more than listens, it can be a weakness as talking blocks a more relevant strength.

While the treasure lies in focusing more on strengths, weaknesses should never be entirely ignored. Generally speaking, a weakness is a lack of ability. The bad news is that every time we use a weakness, the weaker we become. Weaknesses come in two varieties, superficial weaknesses and severe weaknesses. Being nearsighted is a superficial weakness; being totally blind is a severe weakness. Some severe weaknesses cannot be changed because we cannot always put in what Mother Nature left out. Some severe weaknesses are so resistant to change that after a great amount of time and effort, the amount of change is so negligible that it does not represent an adequate return on investment. Severe weaknesses must not be ignored but have to be managed or contained. A blind person needs a white stick, a dog or a helper, or else he or she will fall down a hole or get run over in traffic.

Dr. Hall, as it were, gave people strength identification glasses! People always look better when we focus more on their strengths. If people only see each other's weaknesses, then bad relationships result. If a person wants to end a relationship, all that needs to be done is to keep criticizing! On a positive note, growth begins when blaming ends. Humans have two eyes to enable them to have perspective. When we get to know others, we need to adopt a holistic or total strength approach and be cognizant of both their strengths and their weaknesses as far as their mental, emotional and physical abilities are concerned.

Often in life we have to make choices about what we consider to be priorities. In biology, I chose to study neurons rather than other areas of the body because of my interests in the brain and mental behavior. Out of interest, I discovered that there are neurons in the heart and the gut as well as in the brain. Likewise, I studied business psychology not clinical or educational psychology because of my interest in the commercial world. Psychometrics had more appeal to me than ergonomics. I could go on and on. The main point is that we need to play to our strengths.

Recently I was reminded just how far ahead of his time Dr.

Hall was when he developed his strength-based approach to people in 1940. I came across an article in May 2014 written by Sally Bibb which was headed "Recruit Better With Strengths Based Interviewing." In this article, she points out that the strengths-based interview is "now favoured by everyone from EY and Barclays to Nestlé and Royal Mail. The approach is designed to establish what really makes the candidate tick. Advocates say it helps establish a more mutually beneficial long-term fit, where successful candidates naturally love and thrive in the job." She ends the article by explaining how the strengths-based interview benefits both interviewees and interviewers. Interviewees, she maintains, feel that they are not a good fit for the organization if they receive a rejection letter, rather than considering themselves to be deficient in some way. Interviewers, she thinks, invariably state that they get to know the real person and are confident in the choices they make.

See *References* (p.186) for details of the work of Sir Ken Robinson and Alex Linley on a strengths-based approach to optimizing the growth potential of people.

VISION, VALUE AND VIRTUE DRIVEN

My analysis of Bill's work concluded that he thought successful and significant people are vision, value and virtue driven. At one time, I considered integrating the words vision, value and virtue under one heading, that of integrity. The three terms were integral parts of a greater whole. Vision relates to a person's view of the good he or she cherishes and wants to create. Clarity of vision inspires action. Values relate to the standards a person adopts in the execution of their visions: values shape execution. Virtue relates to the actual activity of making the vision and the values a reality. Whatever visions we aspire to realize and whatever values we embrace, the ultimate test of integrity is actually having the virtue of courage to carry them out. However, in the final analysis, I decided that RSVP was an easier acronym to remember than RSIP and that RSVP also reflects the idea of an invitation from Dr. Hall to which they can respond.

Being vision driven, successful and significant people want to create a better future. President John F. Kennedy in June 1963 in Dublin quoted George Bernard Shaw who said, "Other people see things and say 'Why?' But I dream things that never were and I say 'Why not?'" President Kennedy then went on to say, "The problems of the world cannot possibly be solved by skeptics and cynics, whose horizons are limited by obvious realities. We need men who can dream things that never were and ask 'Why not?'" Am I being like the Man of La Mancha, dreaming an impossible dream when I ask, "What would the world be like if everybody adopted the Hall ways to success and significance – why not?"

For Bill's eighty-ninth birthday in August 1998, I sent him a card on which I had tried to capture his vision in a couple of verses.

Picture a World

Picture a world where each person was fully employed
In doing good things they were good at, intended and passionately enjoyed!

93

A place where due recognition was given and people became
the best they can,
Significance shining in the eyes of every child, woman
and man.

Picture a world where each person was fully engaged
In positively making a difference, whatever their talents,
race, religion or age.
A place where mutual relationships were valued above all.
Welcome to the dreamland of a certain Doctor William E.
Hall.

Being value driven, successful and significant people are
concerned that they behave in a proper, worthwhile, ethical
and moral or right manner. Values are beliefs that are used by
people to evaluate whether things or behaviors are desirable
or not. For successful and significant people, there is no right
way to do the wrong thing, ends do not justify means, and two
wrongs do not make a right. However, Dr. Hall was aware
that just because a person holds a value, while it is his or
her truth, it is not necessarily someone else's truth. What is
self-evident to one person can be questionable to another. Not
everyone thinks that each person is born equal. Often, people
have few or no reasons for the values they adopt. Values can
be passed from one generation to another as truisms, that is,
as values accepted as true without being questioned – self-
evident truths, as it were. In this sense values, are caught not
taught. Sometimes people change their values with regard to
such issues as personal freedom and the right of a woman to
choose to have an abortion, or between equality of education

and the need for positive discrimination or between freedom of speech and the right of politicians to lie without any penalty. I have known people who were against abortion and euthanasia who have changed their position when a member of their family either had an unplanned pregnancy or was dying and experiencing excruciating pain. Values deeply affect behavior. Valuing individual gain more than helping others will shape a person's actions. Simon Cooper, when he was the president of The Ritz-Carlton Hotel Company, said, "People value most the things they can't buy." Bill recognized that most people also want to feel valued. Moreover, he was careful to add value to peoples' lives and not just extract every ounce of value from them!

Being virtue driven, successful and significant people live out their dreams in accord with their values. Virtue requires the courage of one's convictions and the strength to stick to one's principles. Virtue is where the rubber hits the road, as theory is no use to individuals if they do not put it to practice. Virtue is its own reward, as the Greek and Roman Stoics taught. Action unlocks the potential contained in ideas and feelings. George Saunders, author of the New York Times 2014 best seller *Congratulations by the Way* during an interview with Charlie Rose stated that, "An untested virtue is not a virtue."

My study of the works of the Greek philosopher, Aristotle (384-322 BC), particularly his *Nichomachean Ethics* more than likely had a significant influence on the formation of the promise "I seek your greatest good." Aristotle's work was given its title because it was probably edited later by his son, Nichomachus. Aristotle was always talking about various 'goods.' He wrote about the general good which is, for him, whatever is desirable. He also referred to genuine good, which, for him, was what truly perfects a given being by contributing to its authentic growth and development; for instance, genuine good (healthy food) as opposed to apparent good (junk food). Aristotle referred often to the good life and was the most socially-minded of the Greek philosophers; he saw human beings as essentially rational social animals by nature. He maintained that only a life of genuine virtue will make one truly happy, that is, possessing *eudaimonia,* which is having a good or virtuous spirit or sense of well-being; happiness, for him, was an end in itself, not a means to an end.

For Aristotle, virtue stood for excellence at a particular function, and he considered that when practicing the virtues, we should avoid excesses of too much or too little and practice what he called 'the golden mean.' This term is often misunderstood, as people confuse it with the mathematical mean, which is the average. However, for Aristotle, the mean is a point of excellence lying between two extremes, not always in the middle of two extremes! So the virtue of courage, for instance, is a habit of choosing to respond sensibly in the face of danger, avoiding both being reckless on the one hand or being a coward on the other hand. For Aristotle, it was a case of moderation in all things and a caution against adopting extreme positions.

Professor Colin Leach from the university of Connecticut has an interesting argument that individuals' perceptions of themselves or their groups as moral may blind them to their own or their group's immorality. He adopts the philosophy and ethics of Aristotle and his followers, who saw the possession of the moral virtues of righteous indignation, sincerity, modesty, dignity and generosity/munificence as the basis for living a good life and evaluating oneself or others as good. Leach states, "If morality is important to people feeling good about themselves, they will not want to give it up. As a result, the people who see themselves as most moral may be most blinded to their immorality. This is the idea that I have been trying to develop that I call moral mis-engagement – when our sense of our own morality leads us not to disengage our moral system or to rationalise or legitimate immorality, but to actually use our sense of ourselves as moral to go further and to be immoral."

I agree with the Greek philosophers and Dr. Hall, who maintain that good theory is only good theory if it is also good practice. Good moral theories, visions and definitions and classifications of virtues are only worth subscribing to if the end result is moral behavior. Thinking we are moral is definitely not the same as acting morally. My father often asked me what I was going to do next. If ever I said that I was thinking about it, he would snap, "You know what thought does? Nothing!"

POSITIVE APPROACH

For Bill, successful and significant people adopt a positive approach. Nevertheless, he was a realist. What he was for, the opposite he was against. His was never a Pollyanna approach. Pollyannas think they live in the best of all possible worlds no matter what. People addicted to gambling only ever talk about their winnings! In a nutshell, Bill's positive approach inspires people to study good people, recognize good people, and invest in good people. Bill, like Aristotle, used the word "good" a lot. He would ask people to describe a good executive, a good manager, a good salesperson, et cetera. If he were choosing a term today, the equivalent would be the word "great." I am sure that in some way the continued use of the word "good" found an echo in the promise, "I seek your greatest good," with some greatness added.

Bill would have appreciated the story rabbi Harold S. Kushner tells about the Native American tribal chief who informed his braves that inside everybody there were two dogs fighting, one is good (positive) and one is evil (negative). When the braves asked the chief, "Which one wins?" the chief replied, "The one I feed the most!"

Again, Bill took a holistic view of the world, which requires the need to see positives, negatives and neutrals.

Bill, like all good mentors, asked questions and let you work to find the answers, giving a bit of steering here and there, so you thought the answers were totally yours. He was also humble enough to realize that he certainly did not have the answers to all of life's mysteries and that the more a person knows, the wider his or her circumference of ignorance grows. He knew that if he lit someone else's candle from his, there would be more light in the world and that his light would not diminish – in fact, it would be a little brighter. Despite what was said earlier about the mentor often learning more than the protégé, it appears to me that I learned more than Bill did from our relationship.

Bill, like Hugh Austin, had a dry sense of humor. I remember him telling me about a teacher who was complaining about a slow student by stating, "I've taught that boy everything I know, and he's still stupid!"

On another occasion when we were talking about sticking to principles, he told the story about a young man who visited a psychologist. "What is the problem, young man?" the psychologist asked.

"I'm having problems sticking to my high principles," replied the young man.

"I see," said the psychologist. "What you want is for me to help you to develop strength and courage to live by these standards."

"No!" said the young man. "I want you to help me lower my standards!"

Once when we were talking about questions, he told me about a member of the audience who asked him, "Why do psychologists answer questions with questions?" Bill replied, "Why shouldn't we?"

Bill was always trying to bring out the best in others. On one visit, Bill and I were talking about the interplay of reason and emotions. He encouraged me to publish some of my poems. The result was a book called *Hearts Have Reasons*. On another visit when we were engrossed in a discussion about relationships, as previously mentioned, he asked me to think about the key attitudes that were needed to establish trust. The result of that reflection gave rise to the two promises "I mean you no harm; I seek your greatest good," and to the publication of this book.

Recently, I was reflecting on the origin of the promise

"I mean you no harm" and saw an indirect connection between an event Bill and I attended involving the powerful use of the word "harm." When a production of *A Man for All Seasons,* a play written by Robert Bolt, was running in Atlanta, Dr. Hall, Susan and I went to see a performance. At seminary, I had been involved in a production of the play. Although my contribution as the "props" director related to the acquisition of all the materials required apart from costumes, I became engrossed with the dialogue and the acting. The story revolved around the struggle between two powerful friends, Henry VIII of England, who wanted to divorce his first wife, Catherine of Aragon, and marry Ann Boleyn, and Thomas Moore, Chancellor of England, a devout Catholic who, in conscience, opposed the second marriage. Thomas, a brilliant lawyer, had used every legal means he could to avoid taking the oath of succession. Failure to do so would result in the death penalty, so the stakes were high. Thomas was imprisoned and eventually tried. The prosecution, led by Thomas Cromwell, stated that Moore's silence communicated to all that he was opposed to the second marriage. Moore contested that this was not true under the law, as jurisprudence pronounced that in matters of law "silence gives consent." However, in the end, Moore realizes that the court is intent by malpractice to convict him, and when he is accused of being malicious, he declares, "Not so Master Secretary. I am the king's true servant and pray for him and all the realm...I do none harm, I say none harm, I think none harm. And if this be not enough to keep a man alive, in good faith I long not to live."

Those words have been ingrained indelibly in my memory

and still move me today whenever I read or recall them. I embrace their sentiments and try to live up to them in practice.

Like my father and Father Geoffrey Wamsley, Bill died of a brain disease. I visited my father and Bill shortly before they died, my father in 1976 at the age of 66 and Bill in 1998 at the age of 90. They both knew that somebody was there, but I could not be sure that they knew it was me. What I did know was that Bill had been very instrumental in the process that finally gave expression to the words "I mean you no harm; I seek your greatest good."

It's fitting to end this section by briefly considering what my five mentors have in common. Apart from meaning me no harm, seeking my greatest good and being good friends to me, what other factors come into play? We did not always agree, but we never had any bad feelings. Being males and a lot older and wiser than me, perhaps they could, in some way, be seen as substitute fathers. Certainly, my father was away for many of my formative years and subconsciously I might have been searching for a father figure. Certainly, as my brother John stated, we had to be very independent and self-reliant as kids because of the situation in which we found ourselves.

These five role models shared common human characteristics; they were very humble and unassuming. For me, humility is not thinking less of oneself but thinking of oneself less. They all had a great deal of integrity and had an interest in bringing out the best in others by giving or showing the best of themselves. All of these characteristics are ones that I admire in others and would like to have.

In addition, all of them were good at what they did – that is, they were very talented, but they also had an infectious passion for what they did and thereby turned their talents into strengths. Not only did they become excited when they excelled, but they were equally excited when I or others excelled. They were fun to work with, even when the going got tough.

As a child, saints and great people were staple ingredients in my reading menu, and I had an insatiable appetite in this regard, but my mentors were real people with whom I could interact and learn from in real time. I feel very lucky that I was in the right place at the right time to come across such influential people. My mentors definitely were, as William Shakespeare put it in *Much Ado About Nothing*, all "good men and true" and set a good example that I intend to follow as best I can and in my own way, of course.

When learning to meditate, a state can be reached by novices in which they can see their thoughts and feelings passing in front of them: they become, as it were, a detached spectator of their mental life. Another metaphor that is often used to help meditators is to ask them to imagine that the self is the sky and thoughts and feelings just occur like weather below and are allowed to transpire without being judged. Where thoughts, feelings, intentions and dreams originate is very much a mystery.

Many existentialist philosophers would say that at any point in time, human beings' actions are the result of their previous thoughts, feelings and behaviors, especially their choices. We are highly influenced by the relationships we have with other people, particularly role models and mentors who help to shape how we think, feel and behave. In response to the question, "Where did the words, 'I mean you no harm; I seek your greatest good' come from?" I would have to say that they were a spontaneous outcome, an utterance which emanated, as it were, from the culmination of my total life experience prior to their emergence and reflected the sentiments of trustworthy people in my life!

THE MEANING OF TRUST IN THE LIGHT OF THE TEN WORDS

Having completed the attempt to find the origin of the ten words, other questions need to be addressed, the first of which relates to their meaning. From time to time when discussing relationships, people ask me for a definition of trust. I usually introduce them to the sentiments contained in the ten words, as it easier for them to remember them than it is to recall a technical definition. I realize that the ten words are heavily emotionally charged and that there is also a more conceptual perspective that can be taken. This would be a good place to take a rational look at the attitudes that contribute to the establishment of total mutual trust.

Favorable attitudes toward a person can be inferred from verbal or nonverbal responses. These responses can be of a cognitive nature, reflecting perceptions of the self or other person, or beliefs about their likely characteristics; these responses can also be of an emotional nature, representing feelings toward the self or other; and finally, these responses can be of a conative nature, indicating how the person inclines or desires to act toward the self or other person. My main focus when searching for the key attitudes of trust was on the feelings and intentions of those involved and on any actions which follow. My studies of people who were experiencing good relationships confirmed that their intentions were consistently positive. I recall as a student of social psychology observing couples who were in significant relationships and found that they often mirrored each other's physical behaviors, as if they were part of one system. Sometimes they moved in sync and the tone and pitch of voice and eye contact were in harmony.

RELATIONSHIP TRUST

Before exploring the meaning of the ten words, it is useful to consider briefly what is involved in trusting self and others. Trust is assuredly a multifaceted concept.

The first requisite for trust is to establish the trustworthiness of the person to be trusted. Trust begins on cognitive grounds and is related to the degree of certainty the truster has that he or she (in the case of self-trust) or another person will carry out certain specified actions that are in the best interests of the parties concerned. Such knowledge is gained in several ways:

a. Resulting from their prior experience of trust or lack of trust in their lives, people will have a propensity to trust or distrust themselves or others. Some people who were abused as children grow up distrusting others.

b. Resulting from the reliable performance of the specified actions by self or others (competence).

    c. Based on the reputation or the professional credentials of the person to be trusted (technical trust).

    d. By varying combinations of some or all of the above.

Trustworthiness begets trust and, as we have seen, is considered to be central to our evaluation of our own goodness or the goodness of others. Later, we will discuss other characteristics of trustworthy people such as integrity, benevolence, competence and reliability.

Dr. Hall encouraged people to enter into what he called exploratory or inquiry relationships in order to collect adequate data that would enable them to assess the trustworthiness of a person before deciding to enter into a deeper investment relationship. Until sufficient data is obtained, the other person should neither be trusted nor distrusted. If evidence exists that indicates the person is untrustworthy, then a state of distrust is reached and appropriate action needs to be taken. In certain deep and loving relationships, both the truster and the trusted assess each other as being totally trustworthy.

BLIND TRUST, CREDULITY AND GULLIBILITY

When insufficient data exists to assess the trustworthiness of another person, yet the person still chooses to regard him or her as being trustworthy, then a state of blind trust exists. Blind trust increases the risk of the truster being seriously harmed in such a relationship.

When insufficient data or slight or uncertain evidence is presented to assess the trustworthiness of another person and there are clear indications that this person is not trustworthy and still the truster places their trust in him or her, then the truster can be said not only to be in a state of blind trust but also could be described as having credulity. If the person is easily duped or cheated, then they are said to be gullible. In English, the word is similar to gullet or throat, and we see gullible people as being people who will swallow anything hook, line and sinker. Gullible people who have a high level of credulity run a high risk of being seriously hurt in certain relationships. Professional con artists are experts at getting people to trust them as they present themselves at the outset as being exceptionally friendly, likeable and engaging; they smile profusely and can look a person straight in the eye and make him or her believe they are trustworthy. When serious doubts about the trustworthiness of another person arise, it is worth taking due diligence and consulting trusted advisors before making any decisions of any importance that involve this person.

"Doveryai, no proveryai," or "trust, but verify," is an ancient Russian proverb that indicates that while a source of information might be considered reliable, it is worth conducting additional research to verify that such data is accurate. President Ronald Reagan quoted this proverb in December 1987 when signing The Intermediate-Range Nuclear Forces Treaty (INF) with Michael Gorbachev in the White House. However, if you have to verify something, it could not be considered total trust to begin with. A more fitting translation would be, "Trust blindly, but verify."

RISKS AND RELATIONSHIP TRUST

Because human beings are vulnerable and there is no such thing as a perfect person, no human relationships are entirely risk free. Some people take greater risks than others and give people the benefit of the doubt, or a second chance. In some cases, despite a high risk of being let down, some people regardless will place their trust in others; even when let down, they feel that such cases are the exception rather than the rule. Taking calculated risks is safer than using blind trust.

When Dr. Hall asked me to think about the key attitudes that were required for trust, I realized that he was talking about relationship or personal trust, not what I call technical trust. For me, technical trust arises when a person trusts someone whom he or she does not know personally to carry out a function that others have said he or she is qualified to perform. Accordingly, when boarding a plane, most people trust the pilot – or rather, his or her credentials or those who have given the pilot the certificates of competence required. I have heard some psychologists refer to this trust as expertise trust or mastery trust, as it relates to a specific level of knowledge or skill and not necessarily to subjects outside that particular realm.

One day while sitting on board a plane, I was indirectly made aware of technical trust. When the captain emerged from the cockpit and the flight attendant asked him how he was doing, he replied, "Perfect, and getting better!" I was glad to be on his flight!

A GLOBAL CRISIS OF TRUST

Over the last few years, trust and its repair when lost has been a hot topic globally. In the two countries in which I spend the most time, the United Kingdom and the United States, there is a lack of trust in government; voters no longer trust politicians. In January 2014, PressTV reported that, "Trust in the US government has plummeted among Americans amid the US spying crisis, budget woes and numerous problems with the new healthcare law known as Obamacare according to a new survey. Only 37 percent of college-educated adults say they trust US politicians, down sixteen percent compared to the previous year (2013) the survey by Edelman Barland research firm found." On November 14, 2014, the failure of a grand jury to indict, or bring charges against, a white police officer, Darren Wilson, for killing an unarmed black teenager, Michael Brown, in Ferguson, Missouri led the President of the United States, Barack Obama to say "A simmering distrust...exists between too many police departments and too many communities of color." Shortly after this, a Staten Island grand jury failed to indict a white police officer, Daniel Panteleo, who used a chokehold in the arrest of Eric Garner, a black father of six who later died in a hospital, which served to ignite protests in many cities across the United States condemning the overuse of force by police officers.

In the United Kingdom, there has been a focus on a lack of trust by employees in senior managers. In October 2013 in the UK, the Chartered Institute of Personnel Development (CIPD) in its Employee Outlook Survey, Focus on Leadership, which contacted nearly 3,000 employees across the public, private and voluntary sectors stated that one in three employees rate trust in senior managers as being weak. Claire McCartney, research adviser and author of the report comments, "Employees report that trust is the third most important attribute in senior managers (after competency and communication)...with such poor trust scores between employees and senior managers, we must question whether those responsible for hiring are getting the process right." In spring 2014 in the Employee Outlook Survey, Claire McCartney comments, "First, this survey shows a marked increase in negative perceptions of senior managers, with overall trust and confidence in senior managers hitting a two-year low. Trust and confidence levels are particularly low in the public sector..." In other areas of society, trust levels are in decline, particularly because of breaches of trust by people who are supposed to adhere to high standards of behavior. It is disturbing to learn of certain members of the clergy who sexually abuse children or to hear of cases in which financial advisors speculate recklessly with clients' money or of cases of sexual abuse in the military. This crisis of trust is a major concern.

The CIPD was also interested in studying trust and the lack of it in the UK workplace and commissioned Veronica Hope-Hailey, who was at the time professor of Human Resources Management (HRM) at Cass Business School; Dr. Ros Searle, senior lecturer in occupational psychology at the Open University; and Graham Dietz, senior lecturer in HRM at the University of Durham, to explore how organizations can repair trust when it has been damaged. They issued a

- Ensuring that trustworthy behaviors are visibly rewarded
- Encourage leaders to admit mistakes
- Encourage leaders to listen to their intuition to tell whether a leader could be trusted.

At the CIPD Learning and Development Show 2014 at London Olympia in April, Professor Hope-Hailey joined Geoff McDonald from Global Human Resources at Unilever and Bishop Ed Condry, who was responsible for leadership selection and development at the Church of England and Diocese of Salisbury. Hope-Hailey stressed the need for leaders to be personable and straight talkers who, wherever possible, step away from the "uniform of leadership" and reveal their personal side. McDonald stated that "People don't expect perfection, but what they do expect is honesty."

Victor Dulewicz, Emeritus Professor at Henley Business School in the UK, and his team of researchers have recently created a new Propensity to Trust Scale comprising three sub-scales: trusting others, reliability and honesty of others and risk aversion. He is also working on creating Trustworthiness Scales, especially as they relate to doctor-patient relationships and other client-professional provider relationships.

In an article entitled "In Whom We Trust," Hashi Syedain stresses the importance of empathy. He describes how Lorne Armstrong, a partner in the UK consultancy Involve, references some research conducted by the firm that looked at what they regarded to be four widely accepted components of trust, namely reliability, capability, honesty and empathy.

Involve asked businesses to rank these components in order of importance. The results found that reliability and capability came out on top, with honesty placed third and empathy a poor fourth. Yet Involve also discovered that businesses that placed a greater emphasis on empathy reported a lower impact from the 2008 recession on profitability and were less likely to lay people off. Armstrong concludes, "Empathy, which is harder to define and deliver than the other qualities, appears to be the thing that makes the difference."

These researchers, in line with Stephen M. R. Covey, examined the process of trust in its establishment, in its breakdown and in its repair. They stressed that building trust and losing trust is asymmetrical; that is, it is like building a house of cards, which takes much time to erect but can crash in a second. The CIPD article "How Trust Helps" quotes a Dutch saying to capture the speed with which trust can be broken in organizations: "Trust enters on foot but leaves on horseback." The researchers also found out that "faced with economic adversity, those who demonstrated their moral concern for each other not only maintained trust, but, in some cases, actually managed to increase it. Organizations that enjoy such trust may well enjoy higher growth over the next few years than those demonstrating less benevolence."

In the final analysis, I see trust essentially being a decision a person takes to accept that he or she or another person will speak their truth fast and will take certain specified actions for the betterment of those involved. In other words, we accept the other person as being authentic and possessing and practicing prosocial values. In this sense, it could be seen as an act of faith in the integrity of someone to be true to their vision, values and virtuous actions. The ten words represent what I consider to be the main attitudes of total mutual trust and fall neatly into two promises whose meaning can be considered separately but whose total meaning requires their integration.

"I MEAN YOU NO HARM."

This is basically a statement of intent. However, sometimes in complex systems, like human relationships, actions have unintended consequences as the following incident illustrates.

Two good friends, alias Roy and Joan Carter, a married couple, on my recommendation, booked a room at a luxury hotel abroad. I told them that the personalized service provided by employees to guests was second to none. On their return to the United Kingdom, we went for a meal, and I asked them how things had transpired. They told us that they had in overall terms a good time despite a shaky start even though the stay was quite expensive. When pressed about the dodgy start, Roy said he was very impressed by being addressed by name as he emerged from the taxi at the hotel.

"Welcome to our hotel, Mr. and Mrs. Carter. Follow me to the front office. Your bags will be dropped off in your room," said the valet.

Roy also felt that the communication with the bellman who took the cases and with the doorman who next greeted them was first class. The receptionist also addressed them as Mr. and Mrs. Carter. In accordance with due process, before they were given their room keys, the receptionist asked them for their passports and a credit card. The receptionist passed Roy's passport and credit card back to him politely saying, "Thank you, Roy." Joan was then given her passport and the receptionist politely said, "Thank you, Agnes."

As if all hell was let loose, Joan snapped back, "How dare you address me by that name? My mother was the only person to call me by that name. I hate it. It's Mrs. Carter to you from now on. And don't you forget it!"

She snatched her passport and went off in a huff to the restroom to cool down. Roy at this point in his narrative started laughing because he could see the funny side of things now. He then went on to complete the story by relating how the front office manager apologized profusely and offered them free drinks in the lobby lounge, which Roy said went down well and composed them both.

Most likely, the receptionist did not know what hit her and would have been totally taken aback. She was unaware that Joan hated the first name on her passport and, like many people, preferred to use her middle name. Paul McCartney's first name is James. The receptionist did not mean to upset or harm Joan in any way, but she had obviously hit a nerve. Human relationships are complicated because people can and often do hurt each other unintentionally. No doubt the receptionist learned that it is safer to ask people by what name they like to be called at the outset rather than relying on and using the first name on a passport or credit card.

When I was at school, children used to chant, "Sticks and stones may break my bones, but names will never hurt me." It always seemed to me that the children using these words were really hiding emotional scars. People are very sensitive to the names by which they are called. Every one of Dr. Hall's structured interviews begins with a request followed by a question: "Please pronounce your full name and spell it for me. What is the name you like to be called?" Whenever he met strangers or conducted exercises, Dr. Hall would always make sure he knew the name they preferred to be called and how to pronounce it.

The significance of names was brought home to me when I was studying the Gospel of St. John while at seminary. Believers and non-believers have found the opening words of this work to be a very powerful statement. "In the beginning was the Word, and the Word was with God, and the Word was God." During our discussions, the topic of God's name came up. Out of interest, I visited the Jewish virtual library and thought the following clarifying comments are worth considering. "In Jewish thought, a name is not merely an arbitrary designation, a random combination of sounds. The name conveys the nature and essence of the thing named. It represents the history and reputation of the being named. This is not as strange or as unfamiliar a concept as it may seem at full glance. In English, we often refer to a person's reputation as his 'good name...' Because a name represents the reputation of the thing named, a name should be treated with the same respect as the thing's reputation."

However, the main point of the Carter story is to stress that just because we say the words "I mean you no harm" does not mean in real life that we will not hurt somebody accidentally. We are, after all, only human. "I mean you no harm" is the same as saying "I intend not to harm you." The importance of intent when it comes to understanding human actions cannot be overestimated.

The decision to pursue a course of action to reach a goal defines intent. At school, it was drummed into me that one necessary condition for a sin to be a sin is intention. As students, we were constantly being told that the way to Hell was paved by good intentions and bad deeds, and the way to Heaven was paved by good intentions and good deeds. On further examination, intent reveals many fascinating qualities. Interestingly, people tend to judge others by what those others do and judge their own actions by their own intentions! This is known as the false discrimination error. Consistency of intent, that is, determination, is a prerequisite for great performance, which is consistency in practice. The fuel of determination for most people is the elation or emotion experienced from the action taken and of being valued and recognized. Intent is an eye into the future; action brings intent down to earth and turns it into reality. Intent is having the dream; action or virtue is living the dream. However, intent has to be accompanied by corresponding talent and strength. A person can intend to become another Michael Jordan, but if that person does not have the necessary talent and strength, he or she can practice until Hell freezes over and fail to make the grade. Practice only makes perfect when you have the talents and the strengths required.

In his book *The Happy Atheist*, P. Z. Myers has a chapter entitled "Dirty Words," in which he discusses profanity and censorship. He writes, "The most hurtful words I can think of, the phrase that can cause a great deal of pain, are 'I don't love you anymore.' There's not one obscenity in there. Shall we censor talk of love because it might make someone weep?" As you would expect, I, too, find the words "I don't love you anymore," or expressions like them, such as "I hate you," or "I wish you were dead," among the most hurtful words that human beings can use and wish that they would not use them. These words run counter to the sentiments behind the ten words, "I mean you no harm; I seek your greatest good." Human life is made up of pain and pleasure. Not all pain is harmful. The phrase "no pain, no gain" attests to the idea of good pain. Most women who give birth experience pain. Most people suffer pain while dying. Doctors have to administer pain in the pursuit of healing. Parents have to enforce rules or defer their children's immediate gratification in order to attain their children's greatest good. Sacrifices often have to be made in the best interests of others and to create loyalty.

The meaning of the words "I mean you no harm" is not found always in the literal translation of the words because life cannot be lived without ever inflicting physical or emotional pain to achieve a greater good. At times we know that we cannot avoid causing some discomfort or distress. The words "I mean you no harm," in such circumstances, find a cognate of sorts and are a summary of such sentiments as, "If there is any way that I could avoid what I have to do, I would, but there really isn't, so I have to do it." Similarly, when people are angry or otherwise emotionally disturbed, they often say things for effect and their words are not to be taken literally. If they are experiencing abnormal states or having treatment for mental issues, that is another matter. However, in a fit of temper, uttering the words "I wish you were dead" should not be taken absolutely literally. Even the words "I wish I were with the meaning of this song contributed in some way to the unconscious formulation of the ten words, too, as I have listened to *Abbey Road* hundreds of times since it came out. I listened to it again prior to writing this paragraph.

Recently, I had the pleasure of watching a documentary called *Happy*, which sets out to explore what makes people feel happy. One of the contributors is Richard J. Davidson, Ph.D., Professor of Psychology and Psychiatry at the University of Wisconsin-Madison, who, along with colleagues, has for several years been studying the brain activity of Tibetan monks, both in meditative and non-meditative states. For over 2,500 years, Buddhist monks have employed strict training techniques to guide their mental state away from destructive emotions and toward a happier frame of being.

In particular, he has studied the brain of Matthieu Ricard, who has been a Buddhist monk for over thirty years and who has a Ph.D. in molecular biology. At the outset, the researchers studied Matthieu's brain at rest. There were no obvious changes in external behavior. However, when he was instructed to begin the meditation practices specifically designed to cultivate compassion and loving kindness, parts of his brain went on fire, that is, as soon as he *intentionally* generated these states.

Davidson has helped people who have never meditated before to perform such practices over a two-week period and examined their brains at states of rest and when intentionally generating states of compassion. He has found that subjects have increased the size of cortical areas in their brain, not to the extent of a Buddhist master, but to higher levels of happiness for longer periods of time than can be achieved by taking powerful anti-depression medicines. He concludes that through intention alone, without action, we can change our brain. As such, the intention to mean others no harm and seek their greatest good can make us feel happier. However, we will be happier still when we turn the intention into beneficial action.

At the same time, I was reading *Free Will*, written by Sam Harris, another neuroscientist, who concludes, "Thoughts and intentions simply arise in the mind... The illusion of free will is itself an illusion." He thinks that people are the conscious witnesses of their own experience, which is the state meditators talk about, as mentioned earlier. However, in his discussion of moral responsibility, he states that what we condemn in another person is the conscious intention to do harm and asks, "Why is the conscious decision to do harm to another person particularly blameworthy?" To this, he answers, "Because what we do subsequent to conscious planning tends to most fully reflect the global properties of our mind – our beliefs, desires, goals, prejudices, etc. If after weeks of deliberation, library research, and debate with your friends you still decide to kill the king – well, the killing of the king reflects the sort of person you really are. The point is not that you are the ultimate and independent cause of your actions; the point is that, for whatever reason, you have the mind of a regicide." Despite the difficulty involved in establishing the causality and guilt of criminals, Harris recognizes that certain criminals must be incarcerated to prevent them from harming others. He regards psychopaths to be profoundly unlucky in the lottery of life and reminds us that disorders of the brain can trump the best intentions of the mind.

Also in the documentary *Happy*, reference is made to Ogimison, a small village in Okinawa, where per capita the most 100-year-olds of any place in the world live. Moreover, the 100-year-olds are also very happy. One of the secrets they reveal is that, "We feel we should do no harm to others," which is at the heart of the "icharibachode spirit." It seems that to do others no harm is a very positive and a powerful intention.

The first time I came across the phrase "do no harm" was at grammar school when we studied the history of classical Greece. It was attributed to Hippocrates (460 BCE to 375 BCE), the Father of Medicine. The sentiments were first included in his Hippocratic Oath, "I will use my power to help the sick to the best of my ability and judgment. I will abstain from harming or wronging any man by it." However, the actual phrase was used in the Hippocratic Corpus in the Epidemics, "The physician must... 'do no harm' to anyone." Our teacher told us that even today, doctors sign a version of the Hippocratic Oath and that it has become an ethical principle or rule of behavior. During the classroom discussion, there was a lot of confusion about how to treat a tumor. Is more harm done by removing it or by leaving it alone? The vote was fifty-fifty. However, the idea of doing no harm made an impact on me at the time. Recently I learned that Hippocrates died in Larissa, Greece. Totally unaware of this fact, forty years ago, Maureen and I decided to name our daughter Larissa. Perhaps a subconscious influence played a part in this strange coincidence!

Hippocrates was primarily concerned with physical harm, but there are many other ways to do harm to others. We can ignore or shun a person, thereby causing psychological harm. We can talk about others and say things that portray them in a bad light whether the conversation is true or false, defaming their character in the eyes of others. In his book *Subliminal*, referred to earlier, Leornard Mlodinow explores how important social connectedness is to humans, who are essentially social animals. He explains how studies of six-month-old infants, long before they can verbalize attraction or revulsion, are attracted to kind people and repelled by unkind individuals. He goes on to show that when deprived of social connectedness, humans suffer: "It's fascinating that the pain of a stubbed toe and the sting of a stubbed advance share a space in your brain." Indeed, he recounts a study that shows that "Tylenol, it seems, really does reduce the neural response to social rejection."

Also in his book, Mlodinow describes how the hormone and neuro chemical oxytocin promotes trust and is produced when people have positive social contact with others. He outlines studies that show that "volunteers who were given oxytocin rated strangers as appearing more trustworthy and attractive than did others who were not administered the drug." In addition, he goes on to reveal that, "One of the most striking pieces of evidence of our automatic animal nature can be seen in a gene that governs vasopressin receptors in human brains. Scientists who discovered that men who have two copies of a certain form of this gene have fewer vasopressin receptors...are twice as likely to have experienced marital problems or the threat of divorce and half as likely to be married as men who have more vasopressin receptors."

Another scientist who is conducting research into the neurobiology of trust and the role played by oxytocin in the brain is Paul J. Zak, Ph.D., who directs the Center for Neuroeconomics Studies at Claremont Graduate University. He has hopes of helping people who have low oxytocin levels in the brain, such as those suffering from autism or patients with brain lesions in areas normally rich in oxytocin receptors, who have difficulty determining which people appear trustworthy and which people appear untrustworthy. Many neurological and psychiatric disorders involve abnormal social interactions, including schizophrenia, depression, Alzheimer's disease, social anxiety disorder and Huntington's disease, which could be helped by his research.

As a result of my study of comparative religions, history, philosophy and psychology, I found it possible to construct three rules of good relationships.

The Silver Rule: "Do no harm."

Good relationships are defined as those relationships that benefit self and others. The notion of damaging or abusing self and others, in any way, runs counter to the establishment and maintenance of good relationships. The phrase, "do no harm" applies to anyone interested in creating good relationships with another person and goes beyond the medical profession and political practitioners of non-violence.

Much can be learned from advocates of non-violence when it comes to creating social harmony. Martin Luther King, Junior stated, "The modern choice is between non-violence or non-existence." John Lennon declared, "All you need is love," "Give peace a chance," and "Imagine" a better world. Ironically, both were shot to death. A living legend and exemplar of a non-violent approach is the Dalai Lama, who exudes compassion.

It was a revelation to me to learn recently that Nelson Mandela, a man I admire greatly for helping to achieve major social change in South Africa without civil war, was not totally non-violent in his approach. When I heard the news that Mandela had died on December 5, 2013, the words of Martin Luther King flashed through my mind: "If a man hasn't discovered something he will die for, he isn't fit to live." Certainly at his trial in 1963, Mandela made it clear that he was prepared to die to set his people free from Apartheid. It was only by the skin of his teeth that he missed being hanged and was sent to Robben Island to serve a sentence of life imprisonment. Fortunately, this imprisonment was terminated after twenty-seven years in 1990. On the night of Mandela's death, Charlie Rose, a famous American broadcaster and talk show host, dedicated his program to a discussion of Mandela, both the man and the myth. One of his guests, Richard Stengel, an author and a close friend of Mandela, said "I talked a lot about the myth of him being a saint. He hated being called a saint and he wasn't a saint... Ultimately, he was a pragmatic politician. People compared him to Gandhi and people compared him to Martin Luther King, Junior, but he said to me, 'For those men, non-violence was a principle, for me non-violence was a tactic. I used it as long as I was successful, but when it stopped being successful I turned the ANC into a military art of winning because my great goal, my overriding principle was freedom for my people and justice for my people and anything that would get me there was what road I would take.' That is a pragmatic politician, not a saint."

On the following day, I was amused to hear a local reporter in Soweto go one step beyond making Mandela a saint when he said that people there were behaving as if Mandela was going to rise from the dead after three days! One way Mandela kept inspired to stay true to his principles and maintain his inner strength and resilience and face the worst with dignity and defiance was by reciting William Ernest Henley's poem "Invictus," which ends with the lines:

It matters not how straight the gate,
How charged with punishments the scroll.
I am the master of my fate:
The captain of my soul.

It was an even greater revelation to me to read in *The Guardian* internet edition on July 18, 2014 that Arundhati Roy, a Booker prize-winning Indian author, accused Mahatma Gandhi of discrimination. Jason Burke reported that when speaking at Kerala University, Roy described the generally accepted image of Gandhi as a lie and quoted her as saying, "It is time to unveil a few truths about a person whose doctrine of non-violence was based on the acceptance of a most brutal social hierarchy ever known, the caste system." The reporter goes on to write, "Roy's comments are part of a long running historical argument over Gandhi's views on caste." On further investigation, I found out that Roy has recently written the foreword or introduction to a reprint of "Annihilation of Caste," a speech written by Dr. Ambedkar in 1936 but never delivered for political reasons. He did, however, self-publish the speech in order to promote his views. Roy calls her introduction "The Doctor and the Saint," and she sides with Ambedkar, maintaining that Gandhi was essentially the saint of the status quo, insofar as he accepted and wanted to maintain the caste system. In her speeches, she particularly describes in detail how Gandhi thought about and treated untouchables, known as Dalits. Specifically, Roy used Gandhi's description of an ideal untouchable, a Bhanji or latrine cleaner, as evidence of his acceptance of caste roles and considered it to be very patronizing, too. Despite the complex controversy about Gandhi's attitude to the caste system, there is no doubt about the respect Martin Luther King had for the sanitation workers he was supporting in Memphis at the time he was shot.

Even Jesus Christ has recently had his credentials as a peacemaker challenged again. In his book *The Zealot: The Life and Times of Jesus Christ*, published in August 2013, the author, Reza Aslan, paints a picture of Jesus as a rebel rouser who claimed to be the messianic King of the Jews. The Romans tortured and crucified him for charges of sedition especially related to the violence he carried out in the Temple in Jerusalem and for being a pretender to the messianic throne. This is not an entirely new interpretation, although it is somewhat controversial.

Certainly Gandhi rejected the phrase "passive resistance," which he saw as a weakness and advocated "Satyagraha," which means holding on to truth, or truth-force, or firmness in the truth. He was aware that speaking and living our truth can make others uncomfortable and, in that sense, 'hurt' others, even those near and dear who hold different views. Often it takes great courage to be authentic. Despite the discomfort and disturbance experienced by all those involved, there are times when we can no longer hide ourselves and others from the truth as we know it. Certainly, as in the case of determining Gandhi's true position on the question of caste, it is not always easy to establish the actual truth. I remember Dr. Hall stating that anyone who is successful will have to face negative critics. He advised that the true motives of the critic be established at the outset.

At the time of the final edit of this book, the United States Senate Intelligence Committee on December 11, 2014 released its report about the way the Central Intelligence Agency (CIA) handled certain prisoners after the attacks of September 11, 2001. I was shocked to learn of the brutal way some of the prisoners were treated. Obviously, the authorities were not trying to build good relationships with the prisoners, but the harm they inflicted in many cases was excessive, inhuman and not befitting the behavior of members of a civilized nation, to say the least. The report also admitted that such abhorrent treatment of prisoners did not reveal a great deal of useful information. Not that that would ever justify such brutality. It was an act of great courage to be open and self-critical and let the citizens of America and the world know the truth.

On a more positive and optimistic note, it is heartening to consider the research of Steven Pinker, author and psychologist, which is contained in his book, *The Better Angels of Our Nature: Why Violence Has Declined*, published in 2011. Not only did he provide evidence to support his conclusion, but he was of the opinion that human beings may well be living in the most peaceable era in their existence. In an article entitled "A Less Violent World?" which appeared in the November

2014 edition of *The Psychologist*, the monthly magazine of the British Psychological Society, a summary of a presentation Pinker made reinforced his previous conclusions. He was speaking to a body of researchers who had been gathered by the World Health Organization and Cambridge University to discuss whether levels of homicide and other forms of violence could be reduced by 50 percent in 30 years. The reporter wrote that Pinker described this goal as "completely attainable." The article also stated that Pinker presented statistics to show that levels of violence were generally continuing to fall worldwide. The summary mentioned that Pinker did admit that there were some types of violence that might not decline, such as civil wars, violent resistance movements and those seeking human rights in the Islamic world and quoted him as concluding, "Overall, there's a strong realistic, non-romantic case for the possibility of future violence reduction."

It is consoling that someone is taking a big picture view of our world and sees its citizens as generally continuing to do less harm to each other.

The Golden Rule: "Treat others the way you would like to be treated."

This rule is promulgated by Buddhists, Christians, Confucionists, Hindus, Aristotle and Plato. It is also the subject of a magnificent mural in the United Nations building in New York.

The Platinum Rule: "Treat others the way they would like to be treated."

This rule was promoted by Dr. Hall in what he called his "Individualized Approach" personality theme, which addresses a person's level of empathy to the expressed and unexpressed needs of others.

The three rules apply to all our relationships and take account of our sameness and our differences. At the level of our DNA, we are ninety-nine percent alike and members of the same species, *Homo sapiens*. It is because we are highly alike that we can empathize with each other; so the Golden Rule applies. We were all born equal to love and be loved and not to be harmed deliberately; accordingly, the Silver Rule applies. We are also totally unique and special, so the Platinum Rule applies. As Clyde Kluckhohn and Henry A. Murray so aptly put it: "Every man is in certain respects (a) like all other men, (b) like some other men, and (c) like no other man." To which Dr. Hall added, "All at the same time." Every time we relate to people, we have to take account of these similarities and differences in a holistic manner.

My philosophy of life stresses more the unity of things rather than their separation. Self-realization is a search for truth. Violence against self makes complete self-realization impossible. I recently watched a short film, *Hurting to Heal: Exploring Self-Harm and Recovery,* which was funded by the British Psychological Society's 2012 Public Engagement Grants Scheme. The film, produced by HarmLESS Psychotherapy, was launched at the University of Edinburgh on March 1 to coincide with International Self-Injury Day. It came as a big surprise to me that every year around 250,000 people go to accident and emergency departments across the UK due to self-inflicted injuries, and this is only the tip of the iceberg. Dr. Deborah Serani, in her educational blog, describes self-injury as: "A deliberate, non-suicidal behavior that inflicts physical harm on one's body to relieve emotional distress… the clinical term for this behavior is Non-Suicidal Self-Injury (NSSI). NSSI can take many forms from cutting, picking, burning, bruising, puncturing, embedding, scratching or hitting oneself, just to name a few… Statistically speaking, approximately 4% of the population of the United States uses NSSI as a way of coping."

It is also the case that many people psychologically beat themselves up and have low self-esteem, which is also a form of self-harm. So, for me, the words "I mean you no harm; I seek your greatest good" encapsulate the sentiments *I mean myself no harm; I seek my greatest good.* Violence against another person is violence against the self, so it, too, makes self-realization impossible. Brutal dictators, like Stalin and Hitler, destroyed themselves in the process of destroying others. Although Dr. Hall defined a relationship as the response one person makes to the existence of another and a good relationship as one that benefits both parties, my propensity for unity led me to extend his definition to "the responses one person makes to his or her own existence and to the existence of another, which are mutually beneficial." The promises, "I mean you no harm; I seek your greatest good" encompass self-interest because of the unity principle. If we are in some sense one, then helping or harming others will inevitably help or harm ourselves.

Another of the Greek school of Stoic philosophers, Epictetus, born in AD 55, thought that individuals make mistakes about what they can control totally and what they cannot control totally, which cause them harm or suffering. Epictetus taught that we have to learn to exercise our power over the only things that we can control totally: our thoughts and our beliefs. He taught that no one can ever force us to believe something against our will. He maintained that we cannot control totally such things as our mortality, what others think of us, the weather, the past or the future. He reasoned that when we try and inevitably fail to take control of things we cannot control totally, we feel helpless, angry, guilty, anxious or depressed. He also pointed out that when we fail to control the things that only we can control, namely, our thoughts and judgments, we blame our thoughts on others, the past or on fears of the future, among other things, and we become bitter, victimized and feel at the mercy of external circumstances. Resilience and mental health, in his view, come from focusing on what is in our control in a situation, while at the same time recognizing that sometimes we have limited control or limited influence.

Epictetus, like other Stoics, believed in doing what he could to help others. He taught people to do what they could to improve their lives, while appreciating and accepting the limits of their control. Accordingly, if you are in a bad relationship that you cannot change, try to leave it. While you cannot totally control the subconscious functions of your body at a cellular level, you can eat healthy food or partake in an exercise regimen that could help you to live longer. Sometimes you have to wait until situations change and in the meantime use the opportunity to sharpen your inner freedom.

It is somewhat dispiriting to encounter people who see

human beings as violent and totally self-interested by nature. In her book, *A Tale for the Time Being*, referred to earlier, Ruth Ozeki's main character declares, "If you ask me, Japan is not so peaceful, and most people don't really like peace anyway. I believe that in the deepest places in their hearts, people are violent and take pleasure in hurting others." When I was at school, we were taught that people are born with a fallen nature due to the original sin of Adam, which I really felt was unfair but could accept that actions could have unintended consequences. Certainly, the caste system seems to me on first impression to be an unfair way of treating people, but I admit I have not studied it adequately.

I take the view that when humans are born, they receive half their genes from their mother and half from their father with the possibility of certain mutations occurring somewhere in the cycle. Essentially, I sees newborn babies as innocent and good and having the right to be free from harm and entitled to loving care. I recognize that humans are not perfect and that their growth depends greatly on the relationships they have with others.

I like the motivational theory of the American psychologist Abraham Maslow, who maintained that people were motivated to satisfy a hierarchy of needs. He initially postulated that humans have five levels of needs: physiological needs (food, water, sleep, exercise, relaxation, sex and the pleasure of the senses); safety needs (protection from harmful elements, freedom from fear of deprivation and loss of life); social needs (affection, to love and be loved, have good relationships); esteem needs (prestige, reputation, freedom and self-worth); and self-actualization needs (to unlock their full potential).

Maslow, in his seminal 1943 paper, touches on the need to know, understand and appreciate beauty but does not place them in his hierarchy of five, which Hazel Skelsey Guest, a transpersonal psychotherapist, sees as an early recognition by Maslow that his list was incomplete. In an article related to his sixth level, she points out that Maslow posed the question: "If someone is already self-actualizing, what then motivates that person?" Guest explains that Maslow came up with motivation by intrinsic values, which became his sixth level (truth, goodness, beauty, perfection, excellence, simplicity, elegance and so on). She writes "in other words, values that transcend the individual's personal self-interests and for which he coined the term 'B-values.' This is in contrast to the other five motivational levels, all of which involve self-interest in some form or other." Guest also explains how Maslow, after much deliberation and shortly before he died in June 1970, considered all six levels to be biologically rooted. She is correct in noting that most of the literature on Maslow's theory of human motivation, including my reference to his theory in my previous book, overlooks this addition.

As a result, I see humans having the potential to do both good things for themselves and others and also have the potential to put themselves before others and hurt themselves and others in the process, either intentionally or inadvertently. Humans can do what they know is right as well as do what they know is wrong and do so purposely. Human impulses at times need to be controlled if humans are to do no harm to themselves or others.

"I SEEK YOUR GREATEST GOOD"

This promise is an expression of positive generosity and kindness. It is, as it were, the positive side of the intentional attitude coin. It is all about looking for the best interests of self and others. It is all about integrity and benevolence. When we do good things for others, we become better human beings. If someone sets out to use us, abuse us, manipulate or maltreat us, it is not possible to trust them. Once again, it has to be realized that this statement of intent may result in action that, inadvertently, is not seen by the recipient as being in his or her greatest good.

One day after discussing with Dr. Hall how important mutual trust is to the establishment of good relationships, I was relaxing in front of the television, flicking through the channels when I noticed a familiar face. It was the face of Dana, who won the European song contest for Ireland singing "All Kinds of Everything" in Amsterdam in 1970. She was speaking on a religious channel in the United States and telling a story. It was about a little French boy, Pierre, who learned to walk his wheelbarrow across a plank of wood without falling off. He gradually raised the plank until it became necessary to use a rope tied to two walls to gain extra height. Eventually, he could walk his wheelbarrow on a wire between the tops of two very tall trees. Next he joined a circus and became known as 'the high wheelbarrow walker.' One day, an agent asked him if he would like to earn a lot of money by walking his wheelbarrow on a wire outside of the circus. He was told that it would mean going to Canada and walking across Niagara Falls. He agreed and arrangements were made. Pierre asked if he could take his best friend with him and was told that was not a problem.

However, on the day of the event, when he saw the waterfall and heard the thunderous noise of the water, he became very nervous or, as we would say in England, he 'lost his bottle' or lost his courage. His agent was having difficulty persuading him and asked his friend to try. His friend told Pierre that he had no doubt in his friend's ability to do it.

"Are you certain?" Pierre asked.

"Yes," the friend said. "Just imagine the wire as if you are in the circus. The noise is the applause and the crowds are the audience at the circus!"

"Do you believe I can do it?" Pierre asked again earnestly.

"Yes, you have walked your wheelbarrow now for many years. It is second nature for you. The wind is very low, the atmosphere is calm."

"Do you trust me?" asked Pierre.

"Of course, with all my heart," proclaimed the friend.

"Then will you sit in the wheelbarrow while I walk across the falls?" Pierre asked.

Dana smiled and said the answer to that question would reveal how much the friend really trusted Pierre. She never said whether it was a true story or gave the friend's response, but it was a powerful story about mutual trust.

Ultimately, all of the great human virtues culminate and find their best expression in love. That is when humans are at their most noble. So it could be said that "I mean you no harm; I seek your greatest good" means "I love you." However, there are many different forms of love. C.S. Lewis talked of four loves: affection (brotherly love), friendship, Eros (romantic love) and charity (unconditional love). Others talk of sexual love and platonic, or non-sexual love. When I use the term love in this context of total mutual relationship trust, I would see it as unconditional and wide-ranging, as Martin Luther King, Junior pronounced, "When I speak of love, I am not speaking of some sentimental and weak response. I'm not speaking of that force which is just emotional bosh. I am speaking of that force which all of the great religions have seen as the supreme unifying principle of life. Love is somehow the key that unlocks the door which leads to ultimate reality."

While the ten words are general attitudes for total relationship trust, which for me includes both self-trust and trust in particular persons with whom we actually interact, we need to differentiate these notions of trust from generalized trust, which is often the subject of trust surveys. Such surveys ask broad questions like those below that enable people to express their opinions on a five-point scale ranging from strongly agree to strongly disagree.

- *People are more hypocritical than ever.*
- *Given the opportunity, most people would steal if there were no way of being caught.*

Psychologists use these surveys to determine a person's general propensity to trust and classify people into "high trusters" and "low trusters" and correlate their results with other measures such as intelligence and perceived trustworthiness or likeability. Professor Julian B. Rotter and students at the University of Connecticut developed an Interpersonal Trust Scale in the late 1970s consisting of

25 items like those above and found that "high trusters" are happier, more likeable and more trustworthy. However, people who have these generalized dispositions do not trust or distrust others equally. For instance, a man who has a generalized distrust of women because of bad experiences he had during adolescence may still trust his mother, believing she is an exception to the rule.

Obviously, when dealing with strangers, one's general propensity to trust is likely to come into play. "High trusters" are more likely to give the person a chance and give their trust than more suspicious and cautious "low trusters." But even then, many more factors and variables are involved when assessing the potential of someone to be trustworthy. I remember Dr. Hall saying to me, "It is far better to help one person than to have a general love for all humankind." In general terms, he believed that every person has the potential to do something to near-perfect performance, that is, everyone has talent, but each individual has to be studied to discover what that talent is precisely. I remember Dr. Hall telling me that he and Susan visited some children who had extremely low I.Q.s, but he said that, despite this handicap, one particular child was proud of his strength in polishing things so brightly it gave the objects a mirror-like surface.

In relationship trust, what is of prime importance is good one-on-one relationships. If we build total trust with each person in a group or team and each team member does likewise, total team trust can be achieved. Such total team trust will require work by each team member to maintain and sustain their trust, too. If another person believes that you genuinely and sincerely really do mean them no harm and authentically seek their greatest good, it will help greatly in the process of establishing and sustaining relationship trust and in the achievement of total team trust.

Patrick Lencioni, in his bestseller *The Five Dysfunctions of a Team*, emphasizes the importance of trust in teams and sees the number one dysfunction in a team to be the absence of trust. He writes, "Trust lies at the heart of a functioning, cohesive team. Without it, teamwork is all but impossible... In the context of building a team, trust is the confidence among team members that their peers' intentions are good, and that there is no reason to be protective or careful around the group. In essence, teammates must get comfortable being vulnerable with one another...and that their respective vulnerabilities will not be used against them. The vulnerabilities I'm referring to include weaknesses, skill deficiencies, interpersonal shortcomings, mistakes and requests or help... As a result, they can focus their energy and attention on the job at hand, rather on being strategically disingenuous or political with one another." He then goes on to make suggestions for overcoming the absence of trust, which include encouraging personal openness, understanding each team member's personality profile, feedback on performance and experiential team exercises such as those involving outdoor activities, whose benefits he acknowledges do not always translate directly to the working world. He also urges team leaders to create an environment that does not punish vulnerability and warns that "one of the best ways for a leader to lose the trust of a team is to feign vulnerability in order to manipulate the emotions of others." In a complementary guide, *Overcoming the Five Dysfunctions of a Team,* he elaborates his ideas in, what he calls, 'A Field Guide.' He argues that to reveal aspects of one's personal life to others, one gets comfortable about being open with them about other things. In particular, he thinks that if a team member cannot say, "I was wrong," "I made a mistake," "I need help," "I'm not sure," "You're better at this than I am," or "I'm sorry," then the team member will waste time thinking about what he or she should say or having to work out the real intentions of others.

It is my experience that owning up to some flaws establishes trust and helps to bring people onboard. No one likes to work for a know-it-all or an executive who behaves as if he or she is great at everything he or she does. It comes down to the way an imperfection is disclosed as to whether a person is seen as authentic and genuine. On the other hand, care has to be taken to send out the right signals and not expose a fatal flaw, that is, one that suggests a person is not really up to the job. A finance director stating that he cannot read a balance sheet would only encourage feelings of incompetence, not trust. Similarly, phony self-deprecation is not going to fool anyone. The upcoming manager who says "Maybe I set excessively ambitious goals for myself," is really promoting his ego rather than admitting a flaw. Disingenuous revelations will not gain support; rather, they will invite derision or scorn.

As mentioned earlier, an Aristotelian philosopher would interpret the phrase "your greatest good" as your greatest happiness, the joy that flows from fulfilling what is highest or best in your nature. He or she would also point out that it evokes Aristotle's friendship of character (also called a friendship of excellence), which results from virtuous people wishing well for one another. Aristotle referred to two other kinds of friendship, namely, a friendship of pleasure and a friendship of utility. Despite the fact that friendships of excellence will also be pleasant and useful, such factors are incidental, because those involved wish well to their friends for their friends' own sake. Books VIII and IX of the *Nichomachean Ethics* are well worth reading in full to capture the richness of friendship to Aristotle. However, although the Stoics wanted to relieve suffering and Aristotelians wanted to encourage people to lead the good life, one distinction between the Stoics and the Aristotelians is worth noting. For the Stoics, the crucial ethical consideration is choosing between what is and what is not under our control and avoiding getting hurt by things outside of our control. Other people are outside our control, so Stoics are very wary about putting their total trust in another, as they lose some control. Followers of Aristotle, on the other hand, are less individualistic and accept the vulnerability of placing one's trust in another; after all, for Aristotelians, we are indeed social animals.

Seeking a person's greatest good or promoting the good life is a process of helping people to consider options and decide for themselves what is good for them. I am interested in helping people discover how they can achieve what they consider is their greatest good and thereby flourish. Certainly, I try to avoid being morally paternalistic. Rather, I am morally neutral and provide guidelines for consideration. I find it useful to describe how successful and significant people think, feel, and behave and how they differ from average performers or performers who are failing. I also find it helpful to proceed to make some suggestions for people's improvement and growth. However, I am opposed to those who tell people what they *ought* or *must* do in a highly prescribed, dictatorial or rigid manner. To me, this comes across more as "I know what is good for you" than "I seek your greatest good."

In November 2013, after giving a talk at the Lincoln, Nebraska Rotary Club number 14, I was given a leather bookmark which had inscribed upon it:

The 4-Way Test of the things we think, say or do,
  1. Is it true?
  2. Is it fair to all concerned?
  3. Will it build Goodwill and Better Friendships?
  4. Will it be beneficial to all concerned?

For me, a main priority in life is the search for truth. Science is one way to seek the truth in certain domains. For instance, psychology is described as the science of mental life. Many people see science as being certain. However, psychologists make hypotheses and then proceed to see how probable they are of being true. In other words, as scientists, they "hypothesize, but verify." When these hypotheses concern the prediction of human behavior, the acceptable levels of statistical significance required to meet the standards of the British Psychological Society and The American Psychological Society typically fall short of certainty. For instance, when psychologists use various selection methods designed to predict actual job performance, they compare their predictions with measures of actual job performance to see how well they correlate. Do high predictive scores match high levels of job performance and low predictive scores match low levels of job performance? Perfect correlation is 1.00 or 100 percent accuracy, and 0 is no correlation. Figure 1 shows the accuracy of various selection methods likely to be achieved, and the results are quite humbling. As Graveter and Wallnau write, "When judging 'how good' a relationship (between the two variables) is, it is tempting to focus on the numerical value of the correlation (shown in figure 1). For example, a correlation of +0.5 is halfway between 0 and 1.00 and therefore appears to represent a moderate degree of relation. However, a correlation should not be interpreted as a proportion. Although a correlation of 1.00 does mean that there is a 100% predictable relationship between X and Y, a correlation of 0.5 does not mean that you can make predictions with 50% accuracy. To describe how accurately one variable predicts the other, you must square the correlation. Thus, a correlation on figure 1 of $r = +0.5$ provides a coefficient of determination of only $+0.5 \times +0.5 = +0.25$, or 25% accuracy... A coefficient of determination measures the proportion of variability in one variable that can be determined from the relationship with the other variable. Figure 2 provides a graphic representation of the coefficient of determination."

Science can never prove what makes a good life, whether God exists or not, whether there is life after death, whether there is any meaning to life at all, or how we should respond emotionally to situations; for instance, how long a parent should grieve for the death of a child or loved one. Philosophers and proponents of religious beliefs have many different ideas or models of the good life, which people have to consider and decide whether they are convinced or not. The good virtuous life itself involves the freedom to discuss, debate and then choose to pursue a way of life, as long as people tolerate other people's choices to do likewise.

Personnel Selection

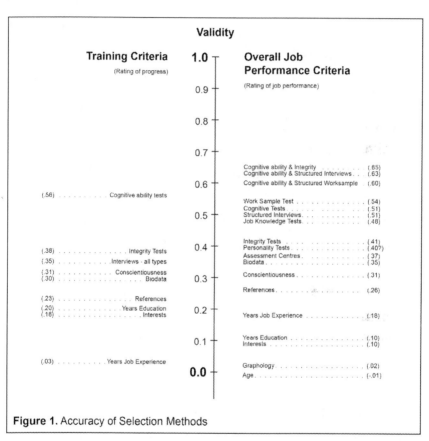

Figure 1. Accuracy of Selection Methods

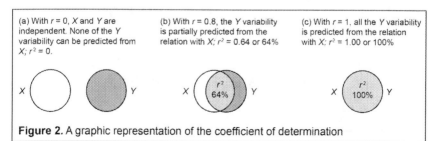

(a) With $r = 0$, X and Y are independent. None of the Y variability can be predicted from X; $r^2 = 0$.

(b) With $r = 0.8$, the Y variability is partially predicted from the relation with X; $r^2 = 0.64$ or 64%

(c) With $r = 1$, all the Y variability is predicted from the relation with X; $r^2 = 1.00$ or 100%

Figure 2. A graphic representation of the coefficient of determination

Stoic philosophy has been used by modern psychological scientists such as Albert Ellis and Aaron Beck to improve the lives of millions of people, particularly by the application of cognitive behavior therapy (CBT). The Stoics reasoned that our emotions are determined by our judgments. Is another person actually behaving badly, or is it more accurate to say that *I* think that the other person ought to do things differently? Many fears are caused by irrational judgments. As previously stated, Stoics maintain that our judgments about the world are all that we can control, and that when we realize this, calmness results. Ellis and Beck found that there are techniques that can be used to bring the unconscious elements of the two-tiered mind (Mlodinow) to a conscious mind level, where they could be analyzed and changed. Ellis and Beck could reveal unconscious habits, make them conscious and then change them as necessary into unconscious habits to improve people's well-being. Philosophy, in this case, has been reinforced by empirical findings.

Dr. Hall's Positive Approach, vibrant in Lincoln, Nebraska in 1947, focused on studying good performers in specific roles by means of empirically sound structured interviews with a view of helping people in these roles to flourish. In recent times, Martin Seligman, who was the president of The American Psychological Association at the turn of the twenty-first century, launched his studies into what the Greeks called *eudaimonia,* or well-being. He collected his data by means of specific questionnaires that were completed by individuals.

The point is that we need to be aware of the limitations of

such scientific methods and measures. There are things that I know with a high degree of certainty, and for the remainder, ranges of probability vary. In many cases, it is necessary for me to embrace living in the mystery.

Scientists often "uncover" truths by looking at familiar things with fresh eyes. A recent example of this is the work of Alan Wallace, a Buddhist monk and scholar who works with the Dalai Lama. He spoke at a conference in London on March 20, 2015. He talks about a new form of intelligence which he calls conative intelligence. He defines conative intelligence as "the ability to judge the desires and intentions that arise and see which ones are really worth pursuing and which aren't, while keeping in mind the old aphorism, 'be careful what you wish for.'" He sees conative intelligence as being as equally important as emotional intelligence.

I enjoy helping empower people to consider the various approaches to leading the virtuous good life and allowing them to examine the options, adapt them as required, and decide for themselves how to move forward and seek what they see as being true and what they see as being for their greatest good. The blunt words of Horace Mann, the great American educator, reformer and abolitionist, remind us also that we are social animals and need to seek the good of others when he said, "Be ashamed to die until you have won some victory for society."

MEANINGFULNESS OF THE TEN WORDS

IN THE BUSINESS WORLD

1996 was coming to an end, and I was working in my office in England putting the finishing touches on my next trip to the United States. The travel agent agreed to move my return trip from San Francisco from midday to late evening to provide more time for any ad hoc meetings on the final day. The trip would include time visiting clients in New York, Washington, working in the corporate office in Lincoln, Nebraska, spending quality time with Bill and Susan Hall, and would finish with client meetings on the West Coast.

Prior to calling a client senior leader, with the analysis of several candidates he was considering for key roles within his organization, I was checking that I had all my ducks in a row with salient comments to support conclusions. The executive I was about to call did not like small talk on the phone. He liked to be brief, to the point and not mince words, as he was operating a busy schedule. Ready, I called him and after relaying my opinions, he thanked me and closed by saying, "When you are next in the region, fix an appointment to see me, as I am having a serious problem with one of our major stakeholders." Later, I spoke to his assistant and arranged to visit his office on my last day in San Francisco.

When we met, he explained that he was having a hard

time pleasing and fully meeting the expectations of the stakeholder, whom he felt was not being entirely open and "beating him up" when results were not precisely to his satisfaction. There were obviously problems relating to clarity of communication, but on examining further root causes, it appeared to me that mutual trust was lacking in their relationship. We became engrossed in a discussion about trust, and he rescheduled his upcoming meetings so that he could go into greater detail. I told him about my mantra of ten words and how he needed to see if he could reach a point where they reflected his sentiments to his stakeholder and be reciprocated. After a lengthy lunch, I left for the airport, glad that I had built some flexibility into my itinerary.

Several weeks went by before I heard from him again. As usual, he was in a hurry and appeared to be just about to board a plane or go into a meeting. He told me that he had been given more responsibility in his company, was having a management conference in Hawaii in April 1997 and that he wanted me to address his senior executives for an hour and explain how working with Talent Plus could be beneficial to them. Without hesitation, I accepted his invitation, even though the terms of reference were quite broad.

When I told my wife and daughter, they were envious. My daughter, Larissa, took me to Rackhams, a department store in Birmingham, and selected a navy blue Pierre Balmain suit for the occasion.

With tongue in cheek I called my talk "Partners in Paradise" and had prepared the necessary slides for use with an overhead projector and made sure I had colored markers and two flipcharts in the room in case impromptu figures or information needed to be presented. I was the second speaker and, as usual, was experiencing butterflies in my stomach as a very confident presenter from JD Power talked eloquently to an earlier PowerPoint exposition of customer satisfaction survey results.

When she finished, my client went to the podium, thanked her for her valuable contribution and stated, "Jim Meehan from Talent Plus is our next speaker. Jim does not really know why he is here."

The butterflies in my stomach at this point started having butterflies of their own. What on earth was going on? Had all my preparations gone to waste? I was about to fall into a panic mode when he related the circumstances of our meeting in San Francisco to the audience. He then stated that, "I have not told Jim what happened after our meeting. I was saving it until today."

He explained that at the next meeting he had with the major stakeholder, things were not going well. They were both in a massive boardroom, seated in the middle and on the opposite sides of an enormous boardroom table, in a pretty adversarial placement and poise. As the agenda was worked through, tension was building to a point where he felt he was being "well and truly beaten up" again. Instinctively, he recounted, he got out of his seat, walked around the table and gave the stakeholder a hug and asked, "Why are you beating me up? I mean you no harm; I seek your greatest good."

Since that moment, he commented, matters have run on an even keel and total mutual trust has been established.

"To celebrate this success, I have asked Jim to come to

talk to you today to help us create a team of total trust. Welcome, Jim Meehan."

If I had not been involved in such an experience, I would have found it hard to believe. The client and his stakeholders were tough-minded, no-nonsense drivers, as "hard as nails" as we say in the United Kingdom, which makes the story all the more remarkable. Since that date, many strong, boiler-maker type leaders who in no way could be considered soft or sentimental when hearing the mantra have commented that they could buy into and adopt an approach based on "I mean you no harm; I seek your greatest good."

IN MY PERSONAL WORLD

Once, after I was asked to read some of my poems, which included "Total Trust," a former colleague approached me and asked permission for her and her husband to read the poem to each other as part of their wedding ceremony. I was later told it was a very moving experience for the bride and groom and for the members of the congregation, too.

A current work colleague and fellow consultant, Mark Epp, agreed to the following insert, which is in his words:

> My mother, Donnie Moselle Epp, grew up extremely poor in the deep South. At the age of eight, she took on the responsibility of raising her two younger siblings while her mother, newly single, worked multiple jobs to bring in enough food just to keep the family alive.

Donnie did not know the meaning of love from her own experience and during my life with her as we grew up, she never said, "I love you." The concept of love was an unknown – how do you express love without an example that is even remotely real? Our relationship was always filled with passionate dialogue and during one of those conversations I quoted Jim Meehan's phrase in terms of building trust, "I mean you no harm; I seek your greatest good." Mom interpreted the response with this statement, "That's the best definition of love I've ever heard."

From that day on, the words "I love you" were spoken by my mom again and again. She had found a way to define something that had always been elusive. And I gained the trust that I knew in my heart was real, but simply needed to hear from her lips. I owe Jim a debt of gratitude and will always think of him as a true friend.

-An experience described by
Mark Epp, 03/01/2013

Recently, Maureen and I went to see the film "Lincoln." We were not at all surprised to see Daniel Day Lewis take the Oscar for his brilliant performance as President Abraham Lincoln. When we were leaving the cinema, Maureen noticed I was in a pensive mood and asked me what was on my mind.

"Didn't you notice what Lincoln said in his second

inaugural address?" I said. "I nearly fell out of my seat. That speech was given in 1864. I know he was trying to unite the nation and appeal to the Southerners. But did you hear what he said?"

"I heard what you heard," Maureen remarked. "But nothing in particular impacted me," she continued.

"He said, 'Malice toward none, with charity for all,' which is as close as you can get to 'I mean you no harm; I seek your greatest good,'" I exclaimed.

As it was the first time I had heard the speech, I could not be accused of plagiarism, and it could be argued the meaning is not precisely the same. However, the sentiments are the same. I was dazed for some time afterwards after seeing this connection. It was like hearing a tune which was almost an echo of a tune you had composed. It reminded me of what psychologists call the "cocktail effect," which arises when someone hears their own name being mentioned despite all the chatter that is going on in the room. Certainly, these words of Lincoln came as a great roar to me. It reminded me of a saying attributed to Mark Twain, "Our ancestors have stolen our greatest ideas."

154

THE FINAL DESTINATION OF THE TEN WORDS

The origin, meaning and meaningfulness of the ten words have been addressed, which leaves one remaining question: "Where are the words going?" Probably a better question is, "Where would I like them to go?" While I recognize that words have a life of their own, I am aware that they can also be helped on their way.

It would be great if in every one-on-one relationship, whether it involved a wife with a husband, a parent with a child, a leader with a follower, a teacher with a student, et cetera, that the ten words could become twenty words as each person addresses them to each other. It would be great if the members in every family, team, group, or association could say the ten words to each other, too, as they could instill in members total mutual trust. Human beings are social animals, and throughout every moment of their lives, they must have at least one person who cares about them and for whom they care.

On several occasions, I have chosen to break a relationship or let it lapse. Sometimes others cause us pain and just want to use us and resist any pressure to provide their motives for such behavior. It requires great humility to realize that the keys to the locks that can open up a person's heart and mind ultimately lie within his or her internal control. Some wounds, such as boils, have to be lanced if they are to be healed. If someone adamantly chooses not to open up on a matter that would negatively affect the well-being of another person, then a good relationship and total mutual trust are put out of reach. Not associating with people who trigger negative reactions within us can be a very important strategy in order to keep balance in our lives. Unfortunately, there are terrorists in this world, and not everyone means us no harm or seeks our greatest good, so we need to take the necessary steps to protect ourselves while still meaning them no harm and still seeking their greatest good.

By consulting, speaking and writing, I am trying to give the ten words wings to add to their legs and hope they will soar as a result. If it is more love that the world wants, and I believe it is, then each of us has some to give. Perhaps the ten words "I mean you no harm; I seek your greatest good" can gain further momentum and turn their intent into appropriate action. While the science of happiness demonstrates that helping others increases personal happiness, we can find solace in the work of Dr. Richard Davidson, referred to earlier, who found that even intending to do something good makes us happier.

When reflecting on the final destination of the ten words, my mind jumped to inscriptions on gravestones. This coincided with some comments made by the Brazilian author, Paulo Coelho, which were included at the end of the edition of *The Alchemist* that I was reading. They were made during an interview conducted by Laura Sheaben for Beliefnet. She asks Paulo, "In your book *Veronika Decides to Die*, Veronika is bored with the sameness of the day. How can people break out of the sameness?"

Paulo answers, "Once someone asked me, 'What do you want to be your epitaph?" So I said, 'Paulo Coelho died while he was alive.' The person said, 'Why this epitaph? Everybody dies when he or she is alive.' I said, 'No, this is not true. The same pattern repeating over and over again, you are not alive anymore. To die alive is to take risks. To pay your price. To do something that sometimes scares you but you should do because you may or you may not like.'"

This, in turn, reminded me of a group training session I attended that ended with the facilitator asking us to write our epitaphs. As I hope to be cremated and thus avoid the need to have an inscription chiseled on a tombstone, I tried to opt out of the exercise and gave the facilitator the best epitaph I had come across. It was carved on the grave of one of my favorite British comedians, Spike Milligan, and read, "I told you I was ill."

Perhaps in the spirit of the exercise and knowing that love and memories never die and feeling slightly guilty, I should have said:

"I meant people no harm; I sought their greatest good.
Sorry to those I did harm or to whom
I could have been kinder.
Thank you to all those who meant
me no harm and sought my
greatest good."

EPILOGUE

Since my early childhood, I have been mesmerized by words in rhyme. I recall in elementary school listening attentively to my teacher reading *The Inchcape Rock* by Robert Southey (1774-1843) and being transported into another world, the world of imagination:

> *No stir in the air, no stir in the sea,*
> *The ship was still as she could be;*
> *Her sail from heaven received no motion;*
> *Her keel was steady in the ocean.*

When thoughts and feelings mean a lot to me, I often express them in rhyming verse, which seems to come naturally. While I enjoy reading blank verse, I am unable to write in that mode. Nor can I write about material objects, which have never excited me. Often I have attended the readings of the American poet laureate, Ted Kooser, who lives not far from Lincoln, Nebraska, and have had the opportunity to talk to this very humble man about his strength in using words to describe objects in amazing detail.

Accordingly, I thought it would be useful to include some poems I have written that reflect the multifaceted aspects of total mutual trust, which at its fullest expression is love. Some of my poems have been criticized for being sentimental, but I agree with David Klein, a philosopher who wrote, "I have never been of the opinion that philosophy and sentiment do not mix. In fact it is the estrangement of ordinary emotions from philosophy that has made much of contemporary academic philosophy irrelevant to us." I would apply his words to poetry, too. Paul McCartney also endorses the use of sentiment when he wrote, "I really don't mind being sentimental. I know a lot of people look on it as uncool. I see it as a pretty valuable asset."

Empathy or Sympathy

"Your wounds deeply wound me."
Emotional empathy mainly.

"You have my pity."
Sympathy to a high degree.

"Your situation is clear to me."
Rational empathy mostly.

"I wouldn't do that if I were you."
Neither of the two.

"I feel your pain."
Emotional empathy in the main.

"You know I see it the way you see it.
You know I feel it the way you feel it.
And I'll help in any way I can."
Now that's real empathy man!

Empathy

If we could listen actively to our every word and sigh,
Would I see you, as you do, and you me as I?

If we could watch each other carefully
when we laugh and cry,
Would I feel as you feel, and you sense as I?

If we could walk in each other's shoes
and not be passers-by,
Would I see the world as you do, and you the world as I?

Active listening and self-disclosure will lead by and by,
To a deeper understanding – seeing more than eye-to-eye.

Armless Hugs

Seeing you there sleeping, I swell with pride.
At such times I've learned to hug you with my hands by my
side.

When away from you traveling world-wide,
Yet again, I've learned to hug you with my arms by your side.

Often yearnings to hold you are denied,
And once more, I turn and hug you with my arms by my side.

Sometimes I realize that I'm not fooling you when I hide
My real emotions and hug you with my arms by my side.

My guilt gives away to your laughter and smiles,
And I am drawn to your arms which are always open wide.

Belonging

What we have, you and I, is something very special,
You know what I mean.
That longing when you're not here,
That longing when you are near.
That longing night and day,
That longing to hear what you say
That longing to feel your touch...

......That longing......

That longing to give you so much,
That longing that you'd hear what I say.
That longing that won't go away,
That longing when you are near,
That longing when you're not here.
You know what I mean.
What we have, you and I, is something very special...

Love

Love is not just an emotion or feeling,
Given only to those we find appealing.

Love is not manipulation or using,
A game of one winning and another losing.

Love is not selfish or grabbing,
A matter of consuming or having.

Love is a process of relating,
The mysterious interdependence of I – other
    celebrating.

A Creed

Confused by conflicting claims of differing religious and
philosophical theories,
We search blindly for the meaning of life.
Perhaps the endeavor would reach an early conclusion if we
abandoned 'isms'
    and 'ologies,'
And just helped people in their daily strife.

Helping others, liked or not, whatever their need,
Could lead to a meaningful humanistic creed.
One which arises from thinking, feeling and acts of charity.
Mixed according to each person's priority!

An Egocentric's Epigram

Some people don't really seem to bother
Living in the world of "I" – "other."
They really appear content to be
In the lonely world of "I" – "me."
Only ever saying "hello"
To their own ego.

Altruism

In order that humans themselves may know,
To others their personality they must show.
It's a journey often fraught with disillusion and toil,
Rejected love into their inner selves makes them recoil.

Introspection is a preoccupation that tends to despair.
So once again, they are forced to leave their egotistic lair.
This time they will more wearily tread, not so easily led
To emulate the ostrich and in their own misery bury their
heads.

Goodness is diffusive of itself.
By others, this goodness will be felt.
As a seed must die before a plant can grow,
So in part, from themselves, humans must outward flow.

Questions of Life and Love

What on earth is the real point of our birth?
To, flourish, what are we supposed to do?
To love and be loved for all we are worth?

Is there a purpose we are meant to serve?
What destination are we heading to?
What on earth is the point of our birth?

Is life over when we breathe our last breath?
How do we avoid feeling sad and blue?
To love and be loved for all we are worth?

What moral compass points to our last berth?
When to sail solo, when part of a crew?
What on earth is the point of our birth?

Why do our kind kill for pieces of turf?
What can stop the pain war victims go through?
To love and be loved for all we are worth?

What do rich and poor folk truly deserve?
Can both become winners in our human zoo?
What on earth is the real point of our birth?
To love and be loved for all we are worth?

You Can't Say it in One

You can say it in two,
"Love you."

You can say it in three,
"I love thee."

You can say it in four,
"I love you more."

You can say it 'til numbers and words have gone.
But you can't say it in one.

Enough is Enough

You have always been my enough.
I never expected you to be perfect.
People are not made of such sweet stuff,
In function or form free from any defect.

Thank you for accepting me as your enough.
For allowing me sometimes to get it wrong.
For selectively calling my bluff,
Whenever my dances did not match my songs.

Enough?

One hug IS enough,
As the anagram shows!
But one hug is never enough.
As far as human nature goes.

Three's a Crowd

Communication is one of humankind's obsessions.
What is needed is less mass media and more two way,
one-to one sessions.

Making Up

Let me plant a kiss in the place where your tears run dry
And in your arms entwine.
Let me wipe the water from your eyes
And be your Valentine.

Heartfelt Empathy

Your pain and joy in my heart.
This is both a skill and an art.

To really feel what you're going through
And see how closely I can come to you.

I'll listen actively to what you say
And, non-judgmentally accept all you convey.

I'll do whatever you require,
Your greatest good is all I desire.

Your sorrows I yearn to take away.
And give you some sun in which to make some hay.

The more of you I understand,
The better fashioned my helping hand.

About Relating

To relate to others I have no doubt,
Unless we go within, we'll go without.
Unless we know how we're feeling and what we're thinking about,
Actions' true meanings we'll never fathom out.
Was that a bribe or was it a gift?
Is that certain smile, really a downer with a facelift?
To relate to others of this I have no doubt,
Unless we go within, we'll go without.

There's More.....

There's more to you than meets the eye,
There's more than tears when you cry.
There's more to you than what you show,
There's more to you than others know,
There's more to words than what is said,
There's more to following than being led.
There's more to kissing than touching lips,
There's more to satire than pointed quips,
There's more to alms than in the giving,
There's more to life than just in living,
There's more to action than the deeds,
There's more to words than what we read.
There's more to you than meets the eye,
There's more to tears when you cry.

F.E.A.R.

False expectations appearing real.
Expectations that make us reel.
Appearing to be sound and true.
Real emotion that makes us blue.

A Citizen of Utopia?

Someone who thinks none harm,
    Wills none harm,
    Says none harm,
    Does none harm?

Someone who in themselves feels warm,
    Is warm,
    To their kind warm,
    To other living things warm,
    To their planet warm?

Someone whose light shines bright and takes delight in
    Sharing their flame,
    Lighting other candles,
    While their brilliance
    Humbly remains the same?

Such people are not mere citizens of our imagination.
They mingle among us and escape our due consideration.

Through Love

Beyond loving there is no greater thing we can do,
When were through loving, then we're through!

Show Your Hand

Babies emerge from the womb into the light,
With fists clenched, locksmith tight.
Let's hope when into their tombs they later slide,
A life of giving has stretched their hands open wide.

Opposites

When very happy, we often cry,
To grow, to self, we must die.
Our bodies are changing, but we are the same.
All around is the permanence of change.
Value from suffering often emanates
Like the perfume of crushed roses or wine from crushed grapes.

Smile Inside

Smile inside! Put a stop to that self-pitying sob!
True happiness is, above all else, an inside job.

Missing You

You are the heart of my life and the life of my heart.
Missing you is the pain of being apart.

The more it hurts
The more love's worth.

If it didn't matter.
It wouldn't matter.

You are the heart of my life and the life of my heart.
Missing you is the pain of being apart.

(Based on words contained in Julian Barnes book "The
Levels of Life," section three "The Loss of Depth.")

Roses in December

I'm glad we've evolved the ability to remember,
So that we, in the North, can have roses in December.
Just think of all the things we might recall,
When in the seasons of our lives we reach the Fall.

Now is the time to fill our memory banks,
By helping others and giving thanks
For the opportunity to do a little good,
And collect one more unforgettable rosebud.

Maternal Trust

With umbilical accord, I floated in the inner space of your womb.
Unheard my first heartbeat signaled life from that silent cocoon.
Wrapped in the warm security of your arms, I first experienced trust in another,
My first feelings flowed freely as they responded to your love, dear mother.

You gave me much freedom as a child, the independence it bred, has served me well.
I was never intimidated by you; to you there was nothing I wouldn't tell.
You even asked my opinion and listened to my infant views.
You trusted me like no-one else and won my trust, something you'll never lose.

Of all the adults in my childhood world, you above all, treated me as an equal.
You told me things just as they were, without layer upon layer of treacle.
When playing cards or other games, you always played to win,
Whether gin rummy, snap, snakes and ladders or ludo, you never gave in.

Your openness enabled me to learn to put myself in others' shoes,
And think twice about how they feel before I would accuse.

Your generosity was all the more, because of the little you have had.
Major sacrifices were made to keep your family fed and clad.

With nervous deafness and speech impaired you have lived for eighty years.
In a world not shared by many, not many have understood your confidence and your fears,
Yet a certain smiling innocence and childlike vulnerability always shine through.
Those who know you, know in your way, you strive to be significant in all you say and do.

Continue to live your life for many years more.
You'll live to be a hundred-that's for sure!
And please remember while you do,
John, Jim, Stephen and Margaret will always love you.

Thank you.

I see poetry as the distillation of thoughts and feelings into words, spoken or written. Despite the power of words to evoke deep sensations and meaning and produce sonic beauty when uttered, they often fail to capture fully the joys and pains of life. Great composers like Lennon, McCartney, Mozart and Verdi combine words and music into songs and operatic arias but, sublime as they are, they, too, only communicate part of the total human experience. How many times do we hear, "Words can't express what I think and feel," or "I am totally at a loss for words," or "You say it best, when you say nothing at all," or variations thereof? Words can be used to suggest possibilities and even allow us to see ourselves not just as human beings but as 'human becomings!'

ACKNOWLEDGMENTS

Much gratitude is extended to the highly industrious and friendly Rhonda Green Whitlow for typing the initial manuscript on a purely voluntary basis and also to Aaron Clark, a work colleague who helped with the photographs and illustrations, as he was a major contributor to the design content of the final cover and totally responsible for its technical graphical representation. Another work colleague to whom I also owe a debt of thanks is Jessi Miller, who used her considerable editing and formatting skills to prepare the final manuscript to meet the highest of professional standards. All three gave their time and talent outside of working hours.

My sincere appreciation goes to all those who have read the text and provided comments, especially Cydney Koukol, Kimberly Shirk and Kris Costello, who are work colleagues. Additionally, I would like to thank Marlene Cupp, one of Maureen's friends, who along with other helpful suggestions recommended inserting maps, and another of Maureen's friends, Breanna Benjamin, who provided useful feedback. Also my thanks go to Paul Lawrence, who provided the photo of Mr. Keene; to Marion Austin, who provided the photo of her late husband, Hugh, and for sharing some documents and anecdotes about his life; to Kevin McGrath, who gave me the photo of Father David O'Callaghan and added a recollection from his mother; and to Daniel Joyce, the archivist at the Birmingham Oratory who provided photos and certain relevant information about Father Geoffrey Wamsley. The help of Rev. John Sharp B.A., M.Th., Ph.D., the archivist of the Roman Catholic Archdiocese of Birmingham in the United Kingdom, is most appreciated for granting access to records relating to Father David O'Callaghan. My gratitude is also extended to my work colleague Mark Epp for his contribution about the meaningfulness of the ten word mantra to his mother.

My thanks go to all those who asked where the words "I mean you no harm; I seek your greatest good" came from, which inspired the writing of the book in the first place.

Finally, I would like to acknowledge the positive influence of the three women in my life: Maureen, my wife, Larissa, my daughter and Pearl, my mother.

Left to right: Maureen (1970), Larissa (2009), and Pearl (1938)

ABOUT THE AUTHOR

Jim Meehan spent his early childhood in Liverpool, England during, and for a few years after, the second half of World War II before moving to Birmingham at the age of six in the winter of 1948. He completed a course in philosophy at Oscott College, where he also studied theology. In November 1967, he began a twenty-three-year career in human resources with Rover Motor Manufacturing Company, the highlights of which were his role as plant personnel manager for Canley Operations in Coventry and his appointment as personnel operations manager for ten international sales companies. During his time with Rover, he attended Aston University, where he obtained his professional qualifications in human resources, a bachelor of arts degree with honors majoring in psychology from the Open University, and a diploma with distinction in the applications of psychology from the University of Wolverhampton, where he later received a master's degree in applied psychology. In 1991, he left the United Kingdom to join Talent Plus, a human resources consultancy with corporate headquarters in Lincoln, Nebraska, where his psychological mentor, Dr. William E. Hall, passed on his life work to him. Since that time, he has provided consultancy services to clients around the globe and acted as an executive coach, a keynote speaker at events and carried out teamwork and team building programs with senior leaders.

Designated a British Chartered Psychologist, an Associate Fellow of the British Psychological Society, and a Practioner Psychologist, Meehan is also a Chartered Scientist and a Fellow of the Chartered Institute of Personnel Development. In addition, he is an associate member of the American Psychological Association and the American Society for Industrial and Organizational Psychology.

In 1994, Meehan and a few colleagues created Outword Trust in the United Kingdom to raise money for good causes worldwide. This charitable trust published Meehan's first two books of poetry, *Hearts Have Reasons* and *Reasons Have Hearts Too.* Second editions were released in the United States in 2000. They are a partial timeline of his life and illustrate the interplay between reason and emotion. His third book of poetry, *Sugar Free Sweet Talk,* was published in the United States in 2009 by Talent Plus, and all proceeds are used to find a cure for diabetes. It is a book written by a person with diabetes for people with diabetes and their caregivers. In 2013, Talent Plus published *Hall Ways to Success and Significance,* a tribute to his psychological mentor Dr. William E. Hall, which can be obtained on Kindle.

Meehan and his wife Maureen have been happily married since 1971.

REFERENCES

Prologue

McCartney, Paul: "The Beatles Anthology" (Chronicle books 2000), p.175.

Meehan, Jim: "Sugar Free Sweet Talk" (Talent Plus 2009), p.23.

Ozeki, Ruth: "A Tale for the Time Being" (Viking 2013), pp.345/346.

Covey, Stephen M. R.: "The Speed of Trust" (Free Press 2006), p.80.

In his work Covey examines the ripple effect of trust, which for him creates five waves: self-trust, relationship trust, market trust and societal trust. He examines how we can increase the intensity of trust and extend trust by using smart trust rather than blind trust.

Covey, Stephen R.: "The 7 Habits of Highly Effective People." (Fireside, Simon and Schuster 1990).

Pope, Alexander: "An Essay on Criticism" (1709).

My Yesterdays

Klein, David: "Travels with Epicurus" (Penguin Books 2013), pp. 72-78.

Mlodinow, Leonard: "Subliminal" (Random House 2012) p.
    51 and pp. 52-78.

Mentors Matter

Khidekal, Marina and Westcote, David: "The Misery
    of Mentoring Milellenials" and "Just the two of us":
    ("Business Week," March 18-24, 2013).

More Than Priests

Whittle, Thomas: Excerpts from letters contained in the
    archives of The Birmingham Roman Catholic Diocese,
    St Chad's Cathedral.
"Sanguine Feat," (The Catholic Herald, November 6, 1970).
Marx, Karl: "The Communist Manifesto," (1848) and "Das
    Capital," (1867-94).
Newman, Cardinal John Henry: "Apologia Pro Vita Sua."
    (1865) and "The Dream of Gerontius," (1865)

More Than a Boss

"The Ocean Cruising Club, The first Fifty Years." OCC
    Publications P.22 & P.299.
Drucker, Peter: "The Effective Executive" (Harper Collins
    1967).
Rodger, Alec; Rawling, Ken: "The Seven Point Plan-New
    Perspectives Fifty Years On" (NFER-Nelson 1985).

More Than a Psychologist

Meehan, Jim: "Hall Ways to Success and Significance" (Talent Plus 2013).

Moorjani, Anita: "Dying to be Me" (Hay House Inc. 2012), p.70.

Alexander, Eben M.D.: "Proof of Heaven" (Simon & Schuster Paperbacks 2012) p.154.

Meehan, Jim: Ibid. pp. 39-40.

Bringle, Robert Ph.D.: "I'm so angry....I could help!" The nature of empathic anger. Oral Presentation Abstract, (Programme & Abstracts of the Annual General Conference 2014 The British Psychological Society) p.50.
Professor Robert Bringle and his team of researchers at the Appalachian State University are conducting some interesting studies which are summarized in the following excerpts from the abstract of a presentation he and a member of his research team made at the Annual General Conference of the BPS held in Birmingham in May 2014.

"Although there are many reasons why individuals help, empathy is very prominent. Empathy typically occurs when an observer has a similar response to a suffering person, and this is usually sadness. Empathic sadness motivates a person to help alleviate the other person's suffering and alleviate one's own discomfort. Most conceptualizations and measures of empathy focus on such sadness-oriented attributes as 'warm,' 'compassionate,' and 'tender.' This research is based on an alternative approach that focuses on empathy as an angry affective response. The differentiation is assumed to occur when the attribution is made about the unfairness of the circumstances that caused the victim's suffering. Whereas anger is often thought to evoke an aggressive response, this analysis examines empathic anger as a basis for helping... Empathic anger provides a means for understanding why some volunteers align with a social justice orientation to service. Having a means to measure the construct will provide an opportunity to study its nature, its development and its journey across time."

Davis, Katy: "The Power of Empathy, Animated." http://www.fastcodesign.com/3023417/ the-power--of-empathy-animated.
The three ideas of connectivity, a separation between empathy and sympathy and hugs are brought together in a brilliant video, "The Power of Empathy, Animated." In her video Katy Davis reinforces the psychology of Dr. Brené Brown. In her video, she uses a sad fox, an empathic bear and a judgmental reindeer and takes excerpts from Brown's popular 2010 TED talk on "The Power of Vulnerability" to make her points.

Bibb, Sally: "Recruit better with strengths based interviewing." (People Management, May 2014) p.34.

Robinson, Ken and Aronica, Lou: "The Element" (Penguin 2009) and "Finding Your Element" (Viking 2013).

Linley, Alex: "Average to A+" (CAPP press 2008) and "The Strengths Book" (CAPP press 2010).

Kennedy, President John, F.: Speech to the Irish Parliament, Dublin June 1963.

Saunders, George: "Congratulations by the Way." (Random House 2014). George Saunders appeared on the Charlie

Rose Show on Wednesday, May 28th aired on the PBS
TV Channel.

Aristotle: "Nichomachean Ethics," (384-322 BC).

Leach, Colin Wayne: "Vicissitudes of (moral) virtue," Social
Psychological Review, Vol.116 No. 1 Spring, 2014 (p.19).
His presentation contained some interesting insights
into morality and virtue, especially when he talked
about the impact of Aristotle's work on the subject.

Kushner, Harold S.: "Living a Life that Matters" (New
York: Knopf 2001) pp. 58/59.

Bolt, Robert: "A Man for All Seasons" (New York: Vintage
International Press, 1960), act 2.

Shakespeare, William: "Much Ado About Nothing" (1598-1599).

The Meaning of Trust in the
Light of the Ten Words

"Survey: Trust in US Government plummets." (PressTV,
January 22, 2014).

Obama, President Barack: "Briefing" (Time Magazine,
December 15, 2014) p.11

"Employee Outlook Surveys. (Chartered Institute of
Personnel Development, October 2013 and spring 2014).

"Where Has All The Trust Gone?" (CIPD report 2012).

"Cultivating Trustworthy Leaders." (CIPD report 2014).

CIPD's L & D Show 2014 at London Olympia April 30- May
1, 2014.

Dulewicz, Victor: "Trust: so important, but can we measure
it?" (Assessment and Development Matters. Vo.5, No. 1
Spring 2013, British Psychological Society), pp.13-15.

Syedain, Hashi; "In Whom We Trust," (People
  Management, January, 2010) p.25.

"How Trust Helps." (People Management, March 2012)
  pp.30-35.

Gospel of Saint John: 1:1, New International Version.

"Significance of names," website-www.
  jewishvirtuallibrary.org.

Myers, P.Z.: "The Happy Atheist" (Pantheon Books New
  York 2013) p.49.

Lennon, John, McCartney, Paul: "Abbey Road album, track
  "O Darling" (1969).

Aldridge, Alan (Ed): "The Beatles Illustrated Lyrics," (A
  Little, Brown Book, 1998), p.191.

Harris, Sam: (Free Press 2012) pp.64, 38, 52/53.

Mlodinow, Leonard: Ibid, p.96.

King, Martin Luther: Detroit, Michigan, 23 June 1963.

Stengel, Richard: "The Charlie Rose Show," October 6, 2013.

Henley, William Ernest: "Invictus," (1875).

Aslan,Reza: "The Zealot: The Life and Times of Jesus
  Christ" (Random House 2014).

Pinker, Steven: "The Better Angels of Our Nature: Why
  Violence Has Declined, (Penguin Group 2011).

"A Less Violent World?" (The Psychologist, vol. no11.
  November 2014) p. 818.

Kluckhohn, Clyde, Murray, Henry A. (Personality in
  Nature, Society and Culture (New York: Knopf, 1953).

Serani, Deborah: www.drdeborahserani.blogspot.com/2012/.

Ozeki, Ruth: Ibid, p.112.

Guest, Hazel Skelsey: "Maslow's Hierarchy of Needs – the

sixth level," (The Psychologist, vol.27, no.12, December 2014) pp. 982-983.

Lewis, C.S: "The Four Loves," (Geoffrey Bles 1960).

King, Martin Luther: "Beyond Vietnam," April 4, 1967.

"Trust and Gullibility," (Psychology Today October 1980), pp.35-40.

Lencioni, Patrick: "The Five Dysfunctions of a Team" (Jossey-Bass 2002) pp. 195-201 and "Overcoming the Five Dysfunctions of a Team" (Jossey-Bass 2002).pp. 13-35.

Graveter, Frederick, J, Wallnau, Larry B.: "Statistics for the Behavioral Sciences, pp. 447-48, West Publishing Company 1991).

Robertson, Ivan T., Smith, Mike; "Personnel Selection" (Journal of Occupational Psychology, 2001, 74, p. 443).

Mann, Horace: Address at Antioch College (1859).

Wallace, Alan: "Mindfulness isn't snake oil," (People Management, February, 2015) pp.40-41.

The Final Destination of the Words

Coelho, Paulo: "The Alchemist" (Harper One, 1988) p.184.

Epilogue

Southey, Robert: "The Inchcape Rock" (1820).

Klein, David: Ibid, pp.95/96.

McCartney, Paul: "The Beatles Anthology." (Chronicle Books 2000) p19.

Barnes, Julian: "The Levels of Life," (Knopf 2013) Section Three; "The Loss of Depth," pp.67-118.

INDEX

FURTHER INFORMATION

As a consultant positive psychologist, Jim Meehan presents keynote speeches and conducts workshops on topics such as good relationships and trust, the power of recognition, investing in strengths, the essentials of senior leadership and the positive approach.

Contact Jim Meehan for more information.

Email: j007meehan@aol.com

Printed in the United States
By Bookmasters